THE NATIVITY QUILT

(A NOVELLA)

BOOK 4 WINSLOW QUILTING MYSTERIES

JAN CERNEY

Copyright © 2018 by Jan Cerney

All rights reserved. No part of this publication may be reproduced, stored in a retrieval system, or transmitted in any form or by any means, electronic, mechanical, recording or otherwise, with the prior written permission of the author.

The characters and events in this book are fictitious. Any similarity to real persons, living or dead, is coincidental and not intended by the author.

The Nativity Quilt

"Oh," Dora moaned, scrunching her short, salt and pepper hair into shape. "Do I have enough energy for anything more?"

She had given little thought to Christmas until Josie called the previous night with a plan. Before then, Milton and she had agreed to have a quiet Christmas together without all the fuss of Christmas preparations. Gifts would be limited to one apiece. She didn't plan on baking cookies for all her neighbors or volunteer to head up holiday functions. Therefore, planning would be minimal. They would attend the candlelight service at the church and then come home to a small ham she'd have prepared in a crock pot. Presents under the artificial Christmas tree would be opened, and eventually they would be off to bed before eleven. She had hoped to spend Christmas day at home unless Julia insisted they come over.

Dora opened the hall closet door, smelling of old shoes, and groaned as she reached down to rummage through the contents. She gingerly sat back on her heels and sighed. So much had happened to her in the last two years while on the sisters' retirement vacation. Neither trip to the far corners of the U.S. had turned out as expected. Besides touring, they had volunteered to search for quilt patterns for the Hedge City, Nebraska, quilting guild. Finding them presented no problem, but the mysteries and people they had met along the way had changed her from a timid spinster to an adventurous married woman.

Thankfully, the only mystery she now encountered was where she put her favorite Christmas quilt patterns. It had been years since she last used them. She massaged her temples to remember. "I know," she burst out in exuberance, straining to upright herself. She redirected her attention to the other hall closet. Struggling with the boxes, she admonished herself for not throwing out unwanted items in a timely manner. Deep within the closet's interior among the mementoes of a lifetime, she pulled out a plastic tote and congratulated herself that she remembered that Josie had convinced her to throw out the ragged box containing the patterns and replace it with a plastic tote with a cover to keep out dust and varmints.

Lugging the tote to the living room, she plopped it down beside her favorite chair. Her half-full coffee cup sat on the end table beside it. Reaching down, she swallowed a few gulps before sitting down and removing the blue lid. As Josie predicted, the contents appeared clean and undisturbed. No dead flies, spiders, or bugs to leave any smudges. The pages of her quilting books had yellowed as well as patterns she had placed in old envelopes to save for later. Unprepared for an emotional reaction, her heart swelled in remembrance of those hours spent with her mother and Josie. It had always been a tradition when she was a child to make the annual Christmas quilt. Her mother taught her two daughters to sew at a young age, and it was expected that each girl contribute to the quilt. The finished annual product took on many shapes and sizes and wasn't always a prize winning quilt, but the girls loved them literally to death for the quilt would cover the girls' beds until they wore away from the washings.

After the sisters' mother died, both Dora and Josie had let the tradition fade. Both had been career women, Dora a teacher and Josie a librarian, and rarely had the energy or time to devote themselves to sewing during such a busy and demanding season. For a few years, they had made table runners or tea cozies for a few special people but other than that the sewing machine remained idle, but Josie suggested they change that and rekindle the old tradition. Dora wasn't sold on the idea, but she didn't want to disappoint Josie.

Dora sorted through the contents, stopping often and calling to mind the quilt pattern and the year it was made. The patterns were simple and suitable for beginning quilters. Ordinarily, her mother never labored over anything too intricate, insisting she had too many other things to do. But the simple quilts they had made lodged a special place in Dora's heart. She counted about six patterns. A few of the patterns they had used more than once. Not one of those quilts had survived. Loved to its last thread, each quilt had warmed and comforted their small family from the time the girls were little through the teen-age years. There were even times when puppies and kittens enjoyed the comfort of the battered quilts.

Reaching in the tote's bottom, she pulled out a brown envelope with no markings on the outside other than a date written in pencil. Turning it over in her hands several times, she opened it and slid out templates of biblical figures cut out of cardboard. No name was given to the quilt nor was there a picture or a sketch of a completed portion. Wondering if it was a quilt intended for a Christmas, she laid out a few of the figure shapes in a row and realized immediately those were the three Wise Men on camels from the East. She hadn't remembered such a quilt, but she would have been a mere child then. But she made a mental note to ask Josie about it when she visited with her again.

As she packed up the tote, she contemplated whether Josie intended to use one of these old patterns or come up with something more challenging. Both she and Josie had become accomplished quilters, learning most of the advanced skills through the quilt guild. She chuckled to herself when remembering Mrs. Wainright of Cooperstown who glorified in appliqué. She would never forget the long hours in helping the dear elderly lady on an appliqué quilt of the New England author homes. She never wanted to face that task again under the time constraints placed on them.

Dora wasn't to wonder too long for Josie called her sister the next day with news. Dora and Josie had been spinsters living together in their parental home until this last fall when they had married two detectives who had solved an art heist on their first retirement trip. Dora and Josie took a retirement vacation to see the United States and collected quilt patterns along the way. For some uncanny reason both sisters were caught up in mysteries in which detectives Milton and Anthony became involved. It wasn't until a year later that they both sisters were married at a Southern plantation to Milton and Anthony.

"I've been thinking," Josie began the conversation.

"Sounds like trouble," Dora answered wryly.

Josie scowled. "Dora, you never change."

"But I have," Dora protested.

"Maybe in some ways. But seriously, hear me out."

"Okay. What's your fabulous idea?"

"I've been discussing plans with Anthony, and he thinks I should come to Hedge City and spend a few weeks to work on our quilt. Would that be okay with you?"

Dora nodded. "We will need to get together. I brought out the tote the other day and revisited our old quilt patterns. They brought back memories."

"I'm sure they did. But I have to admit our quilts wouldn't have fared well in a quilt show."

"Probably not, but the memories have lasted. When are you coming?"

"I was thinking of next week," Josie said. "Would that be too soon?"

"Fine with me. Should I look for more patterns?"

"I'm bringing quilt magazines, and there is always the internet."

"Are we planning on using a new Christmas pattern?"

Josie laughed. "I believe we have advanced in our quilting skills since elementary. I trust the fabric store has an inventory of Christmas fabric."

"Yes, you're right. By the way, I found Wise Men quilt templates in an envelope at the bottom of the tote. No note is made to them anywhere. Do you remember ever starting a quilt and never finishing it?"

"You mean Wise Men as in the Christmas Nativity scene?"

"Yes."

"No, I don't remember such a quilt, but that doesn't mean that we didn't. Why is it important?"

"Oh nothing. I might be developing a mystery instinct."

Josie laughed. "Our parents were just plain people. Don't imagine things that aren't there."

"I suppose you're right." Dora hesitated before she spoke. "There was a date written on the envelope."

"Really? Now you have me curious. What is it?"

"1950."

"You were just little, and I wasn't even born yet. No mystery there. Mother was too busy and didn't even begin the tradition of an annual quilt."

"Sure, makes sense. Never mind I mentioned it. How long will you stay?"

"Until you throw me out."

"It will be day by day." Dora laughed. "Can't wait to see what we can come up with."

"Me too, I need something to do." Josie covered the receiver and muffled something to Anthony. "Got to go, my hubby has a list a mile long to do before I leave for Nebraska. Call you later."

Dora hung up the house phone and finished her dishes. Milton was outdoors completing outdoor tasks to prepare for winter. She agreed to help him before the quilting guild meeting to be held that afternoon in the community center. Too bad Josie couldn't attend, she thought. It would be at this meeting, the members would decide what they would do as a group for Christmas. She secretly hoped whatever they chose didn't involve too much work.

She found Milton outside teetering on a wood ladder putting up Christmas lights. "Milton what are you doing up there?" she screeched.

He smiled under his red stocking cap. "Trying to surprise you."

"You did that." She wrung her hands and peered around for some way to help. "Now please be careful."

He nodded and wiggled the ladder. Her hands flew to steady it. "How can I help?"

"Just feed me the lights as I need them."

"Are these icicle lights?"

"They sure are. Someone told me they are your favorite."

"You've been talking to Alexia."

"I have. She's a sweetheart, and she's very fond of her aunts."

"What made you think of hanging lights?"

"I've never done it before. Have you?"

She handed him several feet of lights. "No, neither Josie nor I wanted to risk our lives".

"We may have a lot of firsts this year."

"Possibly. What did you do to celebrate Christmas?" She asked still holding on to the ladder.

"It was rather simple as I recall. We cracked nuts around the fire. Threw the shells into the wood bin. Mama always baked cookies, not the fancy displays you see nowadays. We enjoyed them no matter how simple they were. Cookies weren't always in the cookie jar when we wanted one, so Christmas was special for goodies. And you?"

She feed him more lights. "About the same. We didn't bother to string lights."

"Do you disapprove of what I'm doing?" He asked without looking at her.

"No, I didn't mean that. I confess I enjoy looking at the lights about town."

"Good. I would hate to be doing this for nothing." He paused while he pounded a few more nails. "Don't cookies and hot cocoa usually follow hanging lights?"

"Does that mean you can do without me while I stir up a batch of cookies?"

"Would you mind? I'm about done here, anyway."

"Any preference as to flavor?"

"Sugar cookies. My favorite."

Dora left him to his task, returned to the kitchen, and quickly sorted through her recipe file for her mother's best cookie recipe. In no time at all the kitchen smelled like a sugar heaven. Milton commented in approval as he came through the door. "Love the smell of baking sugar, butter, and flour. My mouth is already watering."

"The milk is heating. Would instant chocolate mix work for you? I never could get the ratio to cocoa and sugar just right."

"No problem." He reached for the cups out of the slightly yellowing cupboard and poured in the hot milk. Dora removed the first cookie sheet from the oven and set it on the stove to cool slightly before she took the cookies off and set them on a paper towel. Shortly, the couple seated themselves at the round kitchen table and took their first bites of perfection.

"What did your family do for a Christmas tree?" Dora asked Milton while motioning for him to indulge in another cookie.

Milton reached across the table. "Dad usually went out and cut one and dragged it home about a week before Christmas.

"Did you go with him?"

"No, he went alone. I think he thought it was easier that way. And you?"

"We bought ours in town at the grocery store. Not too adventurous but the fragrance of the needles was so divine. It was special to haul it home along with the groceries and the hard Christmas candy, my mother's weakness."

Milton's eyes twinkled. "And what's your Christmas weakness?"

"Candle light church services were always my favorite. We used real candles and fragrant evergreen boughs then. After all that's what a traditional Christmas is about. That and celebrating the Christ child."

"True." Milton scratched his red head awkwardly. "I have been a little remiss over the years." He caught her eyes with his. "I imagine you'll help me change all that?"

"'I'll do my best to give you opportunities. And what is your Christmas weakness?"

Milton held up a half-eaten cookie. "Cookies."

Dora laughed. She had to admit that Milton brightened her days.

Milton scooted back the kitchen chair and finished the rest of his cocoa. "Ready for the lighting ceremony?"

"Shouldn't we wait until dark?"

"I'd rather see if they'll work and fix the problem before the weather turns cold and snowy."

Dora nodded, piled the dishes in the sink, and followed Milton outside. She waited with fingers crossed while he plugged in the lights. The house lit up like a winter wonderland. "I wish the folks could see this. I don't believe this house ever held a brighter holiday display. I love it." She kissed him on the cheek. "Thanks Milton."

"My pleasure, but we aren't done yet."

"What do you mean?"

"The yard looks a little bare, don't you think?"

"Oh, no. You're not thinking of reindeer, snowmen, and dancing elves?"

"Well maybe not the dancing elves." He eyed her warily. "They don't make dancing elves, do they?"

"Here I thought you were a conservative detective, and you're going wild on me."

"Let's go shopping and see what they have for yard décor. I promise not to buy every piece they have for sale."

Dora frowned. She knew she would have a difficult time of squelching his enthusiasm. "I must change my shoes. Meet you at the car."

Dora kicked off her work shoes and padded to the bedroom for her good ones. But on her way, she stopped in the kitchen to answer the phone. "Alexia," she answered. "What's up?" She peered out the window to see if Milton was waiting for her in the car. "We are about to leave for the store. What can I help you with? Tonight? Yes, we will be home. Something important? Sounds intriguing. See you then."

Dora hung up the phone and dashed out to the car. "Sorry, I was detained for a minute. Alexia called and said she has something important to share with us this evening. I wonder what it could be."

―――

Milton had just finished anchoring the reindeer family in the front yard when Alexia drove up. "My, what have you done with this place? I love all the lights." She grinned at her Aunt Dora who was doing her best to be helpful.

"It's all Milton's idea," Dora explained.

"I thought that might be the case. Perhaps I've come at a bad time," Alexia said.

Dora shivered and pulled her sweater around her. "Are you at a stopping point, Milton?"

"Yeah, you two go into the house and I will be there shortly."

Dora held on to Alexia's arm as they climbed the steps into the house. "You've got me wondering what's going on. Want a cup of tea?"

"Please. It's chilly this evening. But what else should we expect this time of year."

Dora placed the tea kettle on the stove and sat down at the table with her niece. "Josie will be here in a few days. Would you want to break the news to us both at the same time?"

"No, it's the good news I don't mind repeating. Josie won't be offended if she's not the first to hear will she?"

Dora shook her head. The teakettle whistled and Dora attended to their tea. She knew Alexia liked the orange flavor and didn't bother to ask her preference.

Alexia wrapped her hands around the warm cup and glanced fondly at her aunt. "I'm pleased to see you and Milton so happy. He seems to get in the Christmas spirit."

"He does and I can't stop him."

Alexia lifted her brow. "You really want to?"

"You know I have never been big on going overboard on anything. I thought we had decided to spend a quiet Christmas together. Josie called and wants to make a Christmas quilt as well. I don't know when we'll have time to do that."

"Oh, dear, and I'm afraid I'll add to your troubles."

Dora reached across and patted her hand. "You are never any trouble."

Alexia winced. "I hope so."

Both ladies turned their attention to the squeak of the backdoor. "The suspense is about to be over," Dora said. "Here comes Milton now." She poured Milton a cup of tea and when he seated himself, she nodded to Josie to begin.

Josie turned to Milton. "Dora's been telling me how her preference for a quiet Christmas may become busier that she had planned. I'm will add to that." She reached into her pocket and pulled out a sparkling ring which she slipped on her finger and held it up for Dora and Milton to see.

"You're engaged?" Dora expelled the question. "I had no idea you were in a serious relationship. Who is he?"

"It's John the same young man you've met before. We've been dating for some time, but he wasn't finished with school yet, so we thought we would wait. However, we want to begin our life together and get married over Christmas. He'll be graduated by then. This doesn't give us much time for planning a wedding, but we'll make it work somehow."

Dora leaned over and pecked Alexia's cheek. "We are both thrilled for you. Now, tell us your wedding details. And you know you can count on us to help you out."

"We have chosen the country church that sits alone on the prairie. It isn't large, so that will cut down on our guest list. A reception at another place will accommodate those who won't be able to attend the wedding."

"Have you set a date?"

"Not for sure." Alexia hesitated. "I will need you and Josie to help."

"Of course," Dora said in her most enthusiastic voice. "Josie loves challenges."

"Please, Aunt Dora. Don't spill the beans. I want to tell her myself."

Dora crossed her heart. "What sort of help are you thinking about?"

Alexia threw her hands up. "I haven't done a thing yet. The daycare takes up most of my time. I don't feel I can leave it in charge of inexperienced personnel." She took a deep breath. "I'm licensed, and I have to adhere to rules."

"I've meant to come by and visit you, but all those children in one place are a little intimidating. How do you do it?"

"I love children. I hope to have a few of my own. "

"You'll be experienced."

"Come by some time and I'll show you around. You'll find out it's not so scary."

Dora wasn't so sure. "Okay, I'll wait for Josie."

"Since you two were recently married, I thought you might have some advice, tips, or suggestions."

Dora glanced at Milton and smiled. "As you know we didn't get married in the traditional venue. Few people chose a plantation mansion, and besides we paid someone to make all the arrangements."

Alexia shrugged. "Any help will be appreciated, and now that I think about it, you were married two for the price of one."

"We were rather brazen weren't we, Milton?"

"Did Josie know you would take advantage of her wedding venue and get married, too?"

"No one had any idea except the minister," Dora said guiltily. "We paid him extra."

"Two weddings I will never forget."

"Do you have your dress yet?"

"No, I thought Mom and you and now Josie would go shopping soon. Since it will be a small wedding, I feel I need nothing too extravagant."

"Have you considered wearing your mother's dress?" Dora suggested.

"Well, no I haven't. It probably wouldn't fit, anyway."

"Try it on and see. Wearing her dress in the country church where we used to go to Sunday school would thrill her to pieces. I know if I had a daughter I would like her to try my wedding dress. Not that I ever had a true wedding dress."

"Aunt Dora you looked lovely in the aqua lace."

"Thanks for saying so. The dress was intended for Josie until she decided she needed something better if she would be married in a mansion." She smiled at Milton. "Wearing a beautiful wedding dress is every girl's dream, except for maybe me."

"I like your suggestion, Dora. Mom's dress was pretty. Both you and Aunt Josie looked beautiful dressed as Mother's bridesmaids. What were you wearing?"

Dora laughed as she pulled out her sister's wedding picture from a bureau drawer. "Billowing pink chiffon. Not really my style, but dear Josie pulled it off rather well."

Alexia giggled. "I loved your pink pill box hats."

"Your mother has always had style. I think they look rather silly now."

Are you planning on an engagement party?"

"I don't believe we'll have time for one. And speaking of time, I'd better run. We'll talk more when Aunt Josie arrives."

"I can't wait for the details," Dora said. "Keep me informed."

———

Josie arrived in time for the Hedge City Quilt Guild meeting. Dora cajoled her into going with her to see what was on the agenda for Christmas. "The ladies will love to see you," she insisted.

"Well okay. I won't be any long term help."

"I know that, and I have to tell you I hope we do something simple this year for Christmas. With Alexia's wedding and our own quilt project we will have enough to do."

"At least you're not bored."

"I should say not, and I'm so glad you're here to help out."

Josie wagged her finger at her sister. "Just be careful what you volunteer me for."

Just as Dora predicted, the quilting ladies greeted Josie with enthusiasm. She saw Josie's eyes well up as each one hugged her. Now because she lived in Iowa she no longer was a quilting sister.

The main topic of the meeting was what the guild should do for Christmas. In the past the group had taken on several charity projects, delivered fruit baskets, or held benefit meals, but this year the guild wanted to do something for the entire community. "I suggest a Christmas quilt show," one member proposed.

"Are we up for such a big project?" the president asked.

"How about we display Christmas quilts past and present? If some of us already have a quilt in the cedar chest, we can use that as long as it has a Christmas theme. Others can make a new quilt." Another member added, "In fact, let's open this up to the entire community."

"And along with that, we could display an avenue of Christmas trees," President Faye commented. "Perhaps we could encourage unique ones. I have seen Christmas trees made from horseshoes, thistles, barbed wire, and the list goes on only limited by creativity."

"Great idea. The men could even get involved in the avenue of trees," Lily said.

Dora's head spun with their ideas. They all sounded good to her but what about a peaceful Christmas? That would not happen. Once they were back at the house, Dora collapsed in the chair opposite Milton. "How are we going to do all this?"

"What's the matter Dora," Milton asked, peering over the newspaper.

"Dora's overwhelmed," Josie explained. "The guild wants a community Christmas quilt show and an avenue of unusual trees. And then there's our quilt project and Alexia's wedding."

Milton nodded. "I see you gals feel you are over your head. I tell you what." Milton snapped his fingers. "Anthony and I will take over the avenue of trees. You make your quilt. We will all pitch in on the wedding and the problem will be solved."

Josie smiled. "Milton what can't you do?"

"I can quilt, bake, decorate, and organize."

"You're hired," Josie squealed in delight. "I wonder if Anthony will pitch in like you promised. He won't be here long, so you will have to work fast."

Milton excused himself for more outdoor work and urged the sisters to begin planning their quilt. "You didn't buy any more lawn ornaments, did you?" Dora asked.

"Not without your approval, dear."

Dora laughed. "I am lucky to have such a wonderful husband," she said when he closed the outside door.

"Yes, you are and don't forget it."

"I'll get the tote from the closet," Dora offered. "Did you bring any patterns with you?"

"Yes, they're in my suitcase. I'll fetch them."

As they sorted through the tote, they stopped at each pattern and reminisced about all the good memories of making the annual Christmas quilt. "I liked the appliquéd Christmas tree," Josie said. "I dreamed every night about the packages I would find there. In fact, I wanted to add presents under the appliquéd ones but, Momma would chastise me and remind me there was more to Christmas than presents. Which one holds the most memories for you, Dora?"

"I loved them all. The snowman was cute and then there's the one with Santa. One year Momma was in a hurry, so we made a pinwheel out of red and green scraps and another year we made one with red and green squares. They were all pretty and so warm on cold nights."

Dora reached into the bottom of the box and showed her the unfamiliar templates. "Do you know anything about these?"

Josie held each one up to the light. "I know nothing about them, but they look like parts of a Nativity scene. Here are a couple that look like shepherds and a sheep."

"Not enough for a Nativity," Dora pointed out.

"You're right. Momma may have made one but quit although it looks like these have been traced around at least once."

"Why would she have kept them if she didn't have the entire set, and why are they still among the patterns?"

She tossed the patterns back in the tote. "I wouldn't fret about it. If you are interested in making a Nativity quilt, there are plenty of patterns online." Josie handed Dora a few of the quilting magazines she brought. "Let's pick out a pattern for our annual quilt."

Determined to use a more difficult pattern than what was in the tote, Josie fanned out the rest of the quilting magazines she had brought. "I've already looked through these, and I'm partial to the poinsettia." She opened a magazine for Dora to see.

"It is pretty and not too difficult. If we get to it tomorrow, we might complete it along with all the other obligations before Christmas. But who gets to keep the quilt?"

"I've got that figured out. A wedding gift for Alexia."

"A great idea, Dora said. "And we could display it at the quilt show. Alexia won't know what we are up to." She felt better about the harried holiday, but she still was curious about the Nativity quilt someone may have made years ago.

The next morning, Dora and Josie drove to the fabric store to buy the fabric they needed for the Christmas quilt. Emma, the proprietor was more than happy to assist. The decision to have a quilt show was a boon to her business. The bell at the door tingled, and quilters crowded the store, pulling bolts of cloth off the shelves and sorting through quilting lengths of material. Emma glanced furtively from one direction to the other. "I hope I ordered enough Christmas print," Emma fretted to Dora and Josie.

There wasn't much decision making for all that the sisters needed were red, white, green, and a print for the backing. After Emma cut the fabric they needed, they left the store. "Emma is elated but frustrated all at the same time," Josie commented. "I hope we made her day."

"We have. I've heard she has had a hard time keeping open. Business hasn't been too good lately. The quilt show ought to help."

"I'm glad. She seems to love what she's doing."

"We'll need another sewing machine," Dora said to Josie. "Before we go home, we'll stop by Julia's and see if we can borrow hers."

"Provided it works. You know how she hates to sew."

Julia was washing dishes when they arrived. "What are you gals up to?" she asked.

Josie poured herself a cup of coffee and sat at the table. "Buying material. I'm sure you heard about the quilt show?"

"I have. You will save some of your time to help with Alexia's wedding?"

"Of course," Dora responded. "She has always been first on our list."

Josie grimaced. "Are you panicking?"

"I am. We haven't much time. She wants the wedding at the old church. It's used less frequently now that we have the new church, so that means it may not be in tip, top shape. We need to check it out and see if it will work for a wedding. You'll go with me, won't you? Pete is out driving truck. He won't be any use to us."

"You bet," Dora volunteered, thinking Julia's husband always had excuses. "What day do you have in mind?"

"Either this afternoon or tomorrow. I must have a venue before we plan." Julia wiped the last dish and sat at the table with her sisters. "Alexia is tied up at the daycare and probably can't come with us."

Josie glanced at Dora. "We were intending to begin our quilt today, but I suppose we could start tomorrow. Can we borrow your sewing machine?"

"Sure," Julia said without waiting for Dora's response. "Meet me at the church in half-an-hour. The sewing machine is in the bedroom closet. Help yourself while I change. Oh, could you stop and get the church key too?"

Dora loaded the machine in the car and drove to her house, unloaded it, and left it on the table. With only a few minutes to spare, she and Josie grabbed a few beverages and headed to the manse.

Luckily, the pastor's wife Denise was home and answered the door when Josie knocked. "Come in, come in," she greeted them enthusiastically. Dora briefly related Alexia's impending wedding, and that she would like to use the old church.

"Oh, dear, I don't know what you'll find. It hasn't been used for a while."

Dora frowned. "We're prepared."

"Would you like a cup of coffee before you go?"

"Thank you," Dora said. "But Julia is waiting for us."

Denise handed her the key. "I'm sure Julia wants to find out what she has to work with. It's been years since a wedding was held there."

"What are we getting ourselves into?" Josie whispered once they had left the manse.

"Don't know. Soon we'll see."

Julia was already at the church when they arrived. She was inspecting the outside of the building. It was in need of paint, but it was the inside that concerned the sisters. Dora jiggled the key in the rusty lock until it clicked. She pushed the warped door open to a stale odor. The floor boards creaked as they walked around the small space to inspect the church pews, the altar, and the windows which were still in good repair.

Josie pointed to a bird's nest occupying one window and made a face to see spiders setting up housekeeping in several of the corners. Luckily, no one saw evidence of mice.

Dora wiped her finger over the dusty pews and the sills. She sneezed several times but didn't comment.

"This isn't as bad as I thought," Julia said.

"And what would be worse?" Dora asked sarcastically.

"Broken windows, missing pew, mice, lots of things," Julia retorted. "Don't worry, Dora. I'll hire someone to do the cleaning."

Dora was about to say she'd be happy to clean, but her aching back told her to keep quiet. She noticed Josie didn't offer her services either. "We'd be happy to help with the food and the decorating," she said.

"I will take you up on that offer. I don't have a lot of time to get everything done," Julia said. "Alexia told me we'd decorate for Christmas using poinsettias, candles, ribbon, and greenery. The Christmas theme will simplify things."

"Has Alexia asked you about wearing your wedding dress?" Dora asked.

"She has tried it on. It needs a few tucks here and there, but she looks beautiful in it."

Dora knew Julia would ask her to do the alterations. She couldn't begrudge the favor for she loved her beautiful blonde niece and would do anything for her. She hadn't counted on cleaning a church either. "Oh Lord, give me strength," she prayed silently.

Julia smiled. "I'll send Alexia over with the dress, so you two can do the alterations."

Josie rolled her eyes. "And where will the reception be?"

"Don't know the answer to that question yet. "Julia glanced around the space one more time. "I'll come back later after the church is cleaned. I imagine you gals are eager to start your quilt?"

"We are," Dora said. "In fact, we will begin once we get home." The sisters waved Julia out of sight, hoping she could find someone to clean the neglected church.

———

"What did you think of the old church as a wedding venue?" Dora asked Josie on their way home.

"It could be romantic once it's cleaned, polished, and decorated. I can see it in my mind's eye. It will suit Alexia well."

"You're probably right. The thoughts of all that cleaning dampened my spirits. Do you suppose we should have volunteered to be part of the cleaning crew?"

"We are old enough to decline. But we may have to clean yet. How many women have time for extra cleaning this time of year?"

Dora sighed. "I never thought of that. Oh, well, guess we'll do what we have to do."

Once they arrived at the house, the sisters lost no time setting up the extra machine next to Dora's sewing machine. They wanted to be close enough, so they could visit while working on the quilt. The first thing they did was to cut out the triangles and squares. Josie couldn't wait to see what a poinsettia block would look like, so she sewed up one when they had cut out enough shapes. She held it up for Dora to see.

"Looks rather simple but pretty. Besides, we don't have enough time for anything complicated."

"Sewing sashes between the blocks with a colorful Christmas print will set off the blocks beautifully," Josie added.

"Alexia will be pleased. That's all that counts."

Josie started the cutting process again. "Will they be giving prizes at the quilt show?"

"I doubt it unless they judge the antique Christmas quilts in one category and the newly crafted quilts in another."

"I wish we had an antique quilt to contribute."

"You know as well as I do that the quilts we had all wore out. They wouldn't be show quilt quality, anyway."

"Are you planning to help with the quilt show set up?"

"I suppose I will if I can find the time."

"I think unusual Christmas trees are intriguing," Josie said.

"I have given thought to it. Recently, I came across an idea in a magazine. I thought I'd run it past Milton." Dora cut a thread. "He would have to make it since it requires sawing."

"You're in luck," Josie said. "He pulled into the driveway, and he's carrying a cake box."

Milton stomped the light snow off his boots outside, placed the box on the table, and called out to Dora.

"We're in here," she answered. "Come and see our quilt."

Milton let out a soft whistle. "I like it. So bright and colorful. I brought you gals a treat." He motioned for them to follow him in the kitchen.

"So what do you have here?" Dora opened the box while Milton put on the tea kettle. "I detect the smell of gingerbread."

"I stopped at a bake sale and couldn't resist. Do you have any whipped cream topping?"

Dora brought out a container from the refrigerator and sliced the gingerbread. When everything was ready, they sat at the kitchen table.

"I have another job," Milton announced. "I ran across Joe from church. He would like help to set up the church Nativity."

Josie took a bite of the gingerbread. "That's so nice of you, Milton. Oh, this is good."

"Might as well. I'm not used to having so much time on my hands."

"It's great you're not out chasing thieves or solving a crime," Dora said. "I might have another project for you if you're willing."

He cocked his head to the side. "Oh?"

25

"Our quilt show will display unique trees, something other than the usual. I've run across an idea in a magazine of using old doors cut in triangle shapes." She snatched the magazine from the counter and turned to the bookmarked page and handed it to Milton. "The door's patina is left as it is, but it can be lightly decorated. A stand will have to be made to keep the tree upright."

"Sounds intriguing. Finding doors may be a problem."

"Old doors are popular now and sell for more money than they're worth," Josie said. "It might be fun to look for them at antique shops or used furniture places."

Dora frowned. "As if we have a lot of extra time. Maybe it's an idea we should skip."

"No, I'd like to try; however, I won't wait for Anthony to help."

―――

That weekend, Julia called in a panic. "I can't find anyone willing to clean the church. Everybody is too busy. What shall I do?"

Dora rolled her eyes at Josie and took a deep breath before she answered. "Don't worry. Josie and I will help. When do you want us there? How about this morning?"

"You signed us up for a job." Josie complained while pressing a quilt block. "Is she going to help us with this quilt? I intended to enjoy this project, but it's turning into another task to be completed before Christmas."

"It's hard not to grumble, but Alexia's wedding should come before our own plans. I suppose we could scrap the annual quilt idea."

"No, besides this is Alexia's gift."

"We could get her something else."

"Let's not give up unless we have to." Josie turned the iron off and put the quilt block aside. "I'd better change into my scrub woman clothes."

Julia had unlocked the church before they arrived. She was already sweeping the board floor. Dora waved away the dust as she entered. Julia appeared as if she were crying. "Now don't get all worked up Julia. We'll get this done in no time." Dora whipped out a large, print handkerchief and tied up her salt and pepper flecked hair. Julia smiled weakly and handed Dora another broom to dislodge the spiders from the ceiling corners and the light fixtures.

After several outbursts of sneezing and coughing, the sisters swept up the worst of the dust. "Let's scrub the floor first to settle the dust and then wipe off the pews and the furniture," Josie suggested.

Two hours later, the women broke for lunch, sampling the sandwiches Julia had picked up at the local fast food place. "Oh, my, I haven't worked this hard for a long time," Josie moaned as she massaged her neck.

"Me, either," Dora agreed while pacing the floor eating her chicken sandwich. She opened a large storage cabinet containing extra hymnals and candlesticks. A box filled with miscellaneous items caught her attention. She pulled it out for closer inspection. To her surprise she saw an envelope marked with the word patterns. Pulling it out, she took it over to Josie. "Look what I found."

Josie dropped her sandwich onto her napkin. "Open it."

Templates like the ones cut out of the same cardboard in Dora's tote tumbled out of the envelope. "Here they are," Dora remarked. She quickly sorted through them.

Julia peered over Dora's shoulder. "What did you find?"

"It's the strangest thing. Similar patterns like these are in my collection of old patterns. Neither Josie nor I can remember where they came from. There are only a few among my patterns and here are more."

Josie lined up the patterns. "I wonder if this is the complete set."

"They look like the Nativity," Julia said, drawn into the mystery.

"What makes it interesting is that the date 1950 was written on my envelope," Dora added.

"That means that whatever we have here was made during our mother's lifetime," Josie concluded. "Is there anyone still living that would know what this was?"

"Most of the town would have been kids. Although, there may be someone in the rest home who knows," Dora said. "Do you think we have the complete set, Josie?"

"I'm not sure, but I can identify Mary and Joseph as being used in two different poses and one angel. Baby Jesus, the manger, shepherds, animals, and perhaps more angels are missing."

Dora pursed her lips. "Whoever worked on this quilt or perhaps a wall hanging had different patterns in their possession. Hard telling where the other patterns are or if they're still in existence."

Josie furrowed her brow. "Dora, you're not thinking of searching for the rest of the patterns, are you? We don't have time for anything else."

"Yes, I know. It's tempting though."

"I hate to break up your fun, but I'm afraid we have polishing to do and windows to wash," Julia reminded them.

28

Before they left for the day, Dora placed the patterns back in the cabinet and posed a question to her sisters. "What do you suppose happened to the Nativity quilt?"

Josie stroked the back of her neck. "We don't even know if there was a Nativity quilt."

―――

The next day, Dora complained to Josie about an aching back while Josie lamented about her sore legs. Both agreed that they were getting too old to be cleaning dusty churches. However, they felt their efforts wouldn't be in vain. With Christmas décor and soft lighting, they both imagined the church would be perfect for Alexia's wedding.

"At least that's done," Dora said to Josie at breakfast.

"Now, how about our quilt?"

Dora yawned. "We have barely just begun, and I have to admit I don't want to work on it today."

"Me, either," Josie agreed. "I have a little shopping to do, and then I will lie down for a nap. We'll just have to work extra hard tomorrow."

"Do your thing. I'm going to putter around the house." But once Josie left, Dora grabbed her coat and her mysterious patterns, left Josie a note without too much explanation, and walked to the rest home. She knew about everyone there and intended to ask questions.

Berta had been a quilter for years. If anyone would know anything it would be her, Dora thought. She searched her out and found her in her room watching television. Dora refreshed her memory about who she was. "I'm Bea Winslow's oldest daughter," she told Berta.

Dora thanked her lucky stars Berta remembered Bea. "Ah, yes, she was older than I. But I remember making a few quilts for charity with her. She was always busy although she helped when she could."

Dora removed the patterns from her purse and showed them to Berta. "I believe these are Nativity patterns I found among my old patterns. Do you remember making a Nativity quilt?" Dora held her breath while waiting for her answer.

"No, I don't remember making such a quilt. I would suspect it was made before my time or by another group of quilters, but wait. I remember there was such a quilt hanging in the church during Christmas."

Dora formed her hands into a prayer. "The church on the hill?"

"Yes, that church."

"What happened to the quilt?"

"I have no idea. I didn't go to the church on the hill."

"Is there anyone else who might have more information?"

"They would have to be older than I am." Berta laughed. "And I am the oldest resident in this rest home."

"Perhaps a descendant might know something. Anyone you could think of?"

"I don't remember all the families, but if you hand me a piece of paper, I could jot down a few names of women that were older than I was. Then you can track down their families if they haven't moved away."

Dora removed a notebook and pen from her purse and handed it to Berta. With some difficulty, she scratched out a couple of names Dora wasn't familiar with. Her visit with Berta had exhausted the elderly lady, and Dora felt Berta knew nothing more. Dora thanked her profusely and left, hoping to arrive home before Josie. Another visit to the church was necessary, she thought, but she didn't want Josie to know what she was up to. No use complicating the situation. At least she had two more leads, and she had confirmed that there had been or was a Nativity quilt somewhere.

―――

    The sisters had been sewing practically all the next day when they heard a commotion on the porch. Alarmed, Dora left her machine to see the cause. "Milton, what do you have there?" she asked when she saw he was the perpetrator of the racket.

"A Christmas tree," he puffed. "Thought I would surprise you. Since you're busy, I didn't think you would mind."

"But I have an artificial tree in the attic."

"I know. I saw it. It's not grand enough for our first Christmas together."

She curled her nose. "But the needles. The mess."

His face turned red. His neck shrank into his collar. "You don't want it? It's nice and fresh."

"Well I... I."

Josie pushed Dora aside. "It smells divine. Bring it in."

Milton glanced at Dora for a cue, but Josie nodded that he should bring the tree in. He hefted it into the living room where their sewing machines sat idle for the moment.

"It will be great to smell the pine while we sew, Dora. It will really put us in the mood. Don't you think?"

Outnumbered, Dora pushed her hair off her forehead and stepped aside.

"Where do you want it, Dora?" Milton asked with a smile.

She pointed to the picture window where her parents always put their tree.

The newly placed Christmas tree released its pungent evergreen odor, and Dora had to admit silently it exuded Christmas. "Now, take care of it, Milton. Water it and vacuum the falling dry needles."

"Oh, I will be happy to. It's been years since I've had a Christmas tree and a real one at that." He stood and admired it like a little boy.

Josie caught Dora's eyes and smiled. "I like a real Christmas tree. Milton loves it."

Warmth rose in Dora's face. She had overreacted and apologized by sharing something she had nearly forgotten. "And it's more than just the fact it's real and fragrant. I read somewhere where cutting down a tree for Christmas is symbolic of Christ's death on the cross. Putting up a tree represents his resurrection and his saving grave for believers from eternal damnation."

"I've never thought of it that way before," Milton said. "What other surprises do you have for me?"

"I'm sure I'll think of something."

"I'll need a tree stand. Do you have one?"

"Yes, there are several in the attic. I haven't used the large one for years, but it should still be there."

"I assume you have ornaments?"

"I do but not enough for such a large tree." She steadied herself as she looked up to the ceiling which needed painting.

"Are they in the attic, too?"

"Yes."

"If you don't mind, I'll bring them down."

Dora sighed. "I have a feeling our sewing is done for the day."

"We've done enough for the day, anyway," Josie said smiling. "I doubt if he will like the ornaments unless you replaced them recently."

Dora frowned. "I saw no need to buy new decorations. Here he comes now."

Milton held a box in one arm and the tree stand in another. "Is this all you have?"

Dora nodded.

"Well, it's not much to work with."

"What did you have in mind?" Dora clipped, forgetting her epiphany momentarily.

"Something traditional."

"You're not suggesting we string popcorn, are you?"

"And cranberries, too." Milton set down the box and tree stand. "Do we have popcorn?" Without waiting for an answer he headed to the kitchen to check.

When he was out of the room, Josie pulled Dora aside. "Now, don't be a stick in the mud. Milton is in the Christmas spirit. Let him have his fun."

"But I don't have time for all these shenanigans. We have a lot to do."

"It'll get done. Just enjoy the moment with your husband."

Milton charged through the living room. "We got popcorn. I'm off to buy cranberries."

"We need string, too," Dora told him as he closed the door on his way out. "He's not even honoring my wishes," she muttered.

Josie laughed. "That's probably for the best."

Dora crossed her arms and frowned. "And to think I call you my sister."

"I'm kidding." Josie picked up her purse and jacket. "I'm off to Julia's, so you two can be alone together."

"We're just stringing popcorn and cranberries. You can stay."

Josie winked. "Sounds like a romantic evening."

Dora waved her away and sat down at the machine, hoping to get some sewing done before Milton returned.

His face was ruddy with cold when he returned with his purchases. Dora turned off the machine and met him in the kitchen. She grinned a cheesy smile. "I'm ready when you are."

"You must think I'm crazy, but it's been awhile since I had an old fashioned Christmas."

"Me too," she said half-heartedly as she pulled two bowls from the cupboard. "Here empty these cranberries into a bowl. I hope we have enough left over popcorn. It works better than freshly popped corn."

"How about popcorn to eat?"

"No problem. I have microwave popcorn unless I'm violating your traditional Christmas."

Milton laughed. "No, go right ahead."

Soon the kitchen filled with the sound of popping corn and a combined scent of fruity cranberries and buttery popcorn. Milton emptied the bag of hot popcorn into a bowl and set it on the table. He sat at the table and waxed a length of string. Then using a large needle he strung one cranberry and then three popcorn. "Where's Josie?"

"Oh, she thought we needed alone time. I invited her to stay."

"Alone time is nice. Don't you think?"

"It would be even better if you built us a fire in the fireplace."

"A cup of tea would be nice, too," Milton added. "Do we have any cookies to go with it?"

"I thought you were eating popcorn, but I might have store-bought cookies. I suppose you'd like me to bake Christmas treats, as well."

"Sure, if you have time."

Something more to add to the list, Dora thought. But how could she stifle her husband's merriment.

It took most of the evening to make the garlands of popcorn and cranberries. Dora had to admit they looked colorful, but her fingers were sore from pushing the needle and string through. Once they were strung on the tree, Dora held up her old ornaments from the box. The faded plastic bells and bulbs didn't complement the homemade garlands at all. "Now what should we do?" Milton asked.

"Search for ideas for handcrafted Christmas decorations. Josie may have suggestions." Dora sighed.

Milton yawned. "I'm off to bed, then. We've done all we can do for one night, and I think I ate too much. Are you coming up with me?"

"I'll be along shortly. I have an idea to explore. Save me a spot."

Milton laughed and kissed her goodnight. Soon she heard the water running and Milton brushing his teeth. She smiled with giddiness. A man in her bathroom. Who would have ever thought?

The Wise Men pattern drew her to the tote. She lifted the lid and removed the cardboard patterns. Wondering what they would look like cut out of fabric, she opened another tote with material and pulled out a plain gold swatch. Carefully, she traced around the pattern and then cut out the first wise man, repeating with two more of the templates. The Wise Men were mounted on their camels on a journey to visit the Christ child not at the Nativity but at a later date when the baby Jesus had grown. The Nativity scene had always intrigued her, and she attempted to envision what the completed Nativity quilt would look like.

Her mother always displayed a small humble Nativity scene in their home at Christmas. The recreated stable and the figures were not expensive but made of cardboard. Both she and Josie had kept that tradition going every Christmas, using the same faded crèche.

Before she resigned herself to bed, she studied the tree with its home made garland trim. She appreciated the lights, but what did the tree require to complete the traditional look? Thinking back to the trees of her childhood, she remembered making ginger bread ornaments. "That's it," she whispered to herself. Another thing to do, but she had to admit Milton had stirred the Christmas spirit in her.

———

Every Sunday morning since they had married, Dora usually found Milton in the kitchen preparing breakfast. This Sunday morning was no different. He was humming a Christmas carol while frying bacon and eggs.

"I've never seen you so cheerful," Dora said, sitting down at the table with a cup of coffee.

"What have we to be glum about? Jesus came into the world to save us from our sin and give us eternal life. That's pure joy, a fruit of the Spirit."

"Yes, he did. Thanks for reminding me. I don't meditate on his saving grace enough."

Milton set breakfast on the table and poured another round of coffee. "Christ is Christmas. Too many forget this truth."

"And I've been trying to squelch your enthusiasm, Milton. I'm sorry."

He patted her hand. "No need to worry. You're coming around, aren't you?"

"I am. I've always had a negative side that has kept me from rejoicing every single day, but I think you will help me change that."

Milton leaned across the table and kissed her.

Josie, still dressed in her robe, joined them at the table, yawning. "Oh, excuse me. You should have gotten me up."

"I thought the smell of bacon and coffee would do the job," Milton chuckled, slightly embarrassed.

"It did. Thanks for this amazing breakfast."

Dora passed her the toast. "You apparently came in late last night. I didn't hear you."

"I did. I was helping Julia and Alexia with wedding plans. Time got away from us."

"Anything new to report?"

"We discussed the reception." Josie paused. "Julia is having a difficult time booking a venue with all the Christmas parties and such. Even the church basement is in the middle of renovation."

"No ideas at all," Dora asked.

"We kicked a few around. Like using Julia's home or yours."

"My house for a reception? It isn't big enough for a wedding reception."

"That's what I told Julia."

"I'm thinking Alexia should have chosen another date."

"Too late now. We must accommodate her somehow."

"Will you go to church with us?" Dora asked.

"Sure, a hot shower should wake me up."

Dora stacked the dirty plates. "It's all yours, Milton. All I have to do is dress. Need help with dishes?"

"No, got it covered."

In an hour, the threesome entered the church, shook hands with the greeters, and sat down to peruse the church bulletin. At the end of the weekly announcements was a section asking for volunteers. Josie pointed it out to Dora's attention. "Anything you're interested in?" she whispered. Dora frowned and then remembered her promise to Milton. She read where the church needed someone to set up the Christmas tree and decorate it, someone to help with the Christmas program, someone to sing at the annual cantata, and someone to visit to the rest home. Dora hadn't intended to become involved with anymore activities. She guiltily closed the bulletin and located the first song in the church hymnal and waited for church to begin.

After the benediction, the parishioners filed out of the church, shook hands with the pastor, and gathered in the foyer to visit. Two of Dora's church friends cornered her before she could slip out the door.

"Dora, we're having trouble finding volunteers for certain projects. I'm sure you read the list of wanted help."

"I have, but I'm so busy. I'm sure you have heard my niece is getting married. We don't have a lot of time for preparations. Josie is here, and we are making a quilt for Alexia. I don't know where I'd find the time." Dora rambled on each time they attempted to persuade her to join them. By the end of the conversation, she had agreed to sing at the Cantata and visit the rest home.

Milton waited for her outside the church and inquired to where she had been. "I've been volunteering," she said, attempting to sound cheerful.

―――――

Josie had promised that she would pick up the slack with the quilt while Dora worked at her commitments. "You have a lovely voice, Dora, you should share it. And you are good with elderly people. They have to be lonely."

Dora knew she hadn't been serving God and the church as she should. There was always an excuse to become involved. She had taken off two years to enjoy herself and hadn't been a part of her church at all. Volunteers were hard to find, especially this time of year.

While Josie was sewing, Dora made a few calls to the other members who had planned to visit the rest home with her. They arranged to meet at the church in a week to make food baskets to give to the rest home residents. She wrote the date on the calendar which was rapidly filling up with errands, appointments, and commitments, reminding her everything written there was important. Her image of a quiet Christmas was fast disappearing.

The cantata was first on her list. Practice would begin tomorrow night. She had invited Josie to join her, but she begged off. "My voice is terrible. What are you thinking?" Josie had told her. But there was Milton who sang beside her in church on Sundays. She thought he might agree. Male participants were hard to recruit, but since he was enthusiastic about Christmas, he might relent. After her phone calls, she assumed her position at the sewing machine. Josie was making good progress.

Dora held up a finished block. "This promises to be a beautiful quilt. I hope to complete a block before lunch."

"Have you given anymore thought to the Nativity quilt?"

"I have had little time to think about it. Do you have any ideas where we could find the rest of the templates?"

"You haven't talked to any more quilters?"

Dora shook her head. "I fear the original quilters are all gone. I have to do more searching."

"How about the church? Not the prairie church but the one we attend. There could be a scrapbook, photographs, or some mention of a Nativity quilt. I would think it would have been worthy of mention."

"Good idea. I'll do that before cantata practice tomorrow."

"Have you found anyone to ride with?"

"I'm thinking of asking Milton at lunch. He has a fair voice."

"Good idea. What's for lunch?"

"Sandwiches. Milton's picking up the fixings. In fact, I hear him now."

Both sisters shut off their machines and met him in the kitchen where they laid out the cold cuts, tomatoes, lettuce, and mayonnaise. Milton had news. "One of the guys downtown asked me to join the cantata."

"Are you?" Dora asked.

"I think I could handle it. I stay on key."

Dora smiled. "You do, and I was about to ask you."

"Great. We can go together and sing our hearts out."

She stood on her tip-toes and looked into his eyes. "Milton, dear, you cease to amaze me."

The next afternoon, Dora informed Milton that she wanted to arrive at the church early to search for evidence of the Nativity quilt made over fifty years ago.

"Do you really think you can find proof of a quilt made that long ago?" he asked.

"Perhaps not the quilt, but I've found a few patterns. I'd like to find more."

"For what reason?"

"I'm not sure; maybe a connection with my mother. She made simple quilts with us." She paused. "Strange how I only thought of my mother as a mother, not as a member of a guild or an integral part of church, or a wife."

"I understand. I also have a strong connection to my past. It makes us what we are today." Milton chucked her under the chin before he backed the car out of the garage. As soon as they arrived at the church, Dora turned the light on in the library and searched. Milton helped even though he told her he wasn't sure what he was looking for. Both perused a stack of scrapbooks which had turned yellow and brittle with age but discovered a picture of her mother with a group of women, but there was no evidence of a quilt. Dora closed the book in defeat.

"Wait Dora. Did you know who the women were with your mother?"

"I didn't pay attention."

"Open the book and find the photo and see if you can identify them."

She did as he said and opened the book to the less than clear photograph. "I wish I had a magnifying glass." Dora squinted and recognized the women who were young in the

41

photo. She remembered them as being older when she was a young girl. She feared all of them were deceased except for one woman whom she couldn't remember. "Milton, use your phone and take a picture of this. I'll show it around and see if anyone recognizes this lady." She pointed to a fuzzy image of a much younger woman.

After cantata practice, Dora asked several of the older women if they could identify the woman in the photo. All said they did not know her and even admitted there were few they could identify. It had been too many years ago, and besides some families had moved. Milton reassured Dora not to give up. Someone had to know who she was.

Dora nodded in agreement. Many town people came out for cantata practice. Dora tucked herself in the alto section, and Milton found a place with the bass. The conductor gave them an overview of what they would sing and even included several selections from Handel's Messiah. It had been years since Dora took part in a musical tribute to Christmas. Milton looked so handsome to her, holding the music and singing with gusto. He caught her gaze and smiled. She blushed. Being married to Milton had been an adventure. She never knew he was so talented.

A warm feeling enveloped her. With him helping her, she felt confident she would find the whereabouts of the Nativity quilt. She was certain he would never let her down.

———

Dora and Josie hadn't planned on setting up the church's Christmas tree until Dora received a frantic call the next morning from the minister's wife informing them the person in charge had turned her ankle on the ice and couldn't do it.

Dora had her cookbooks and recipe cards splayed out on the kitchen table. She had planned on baking while Josie sewed. Neither sister could think up an excuse why they couldn't put up the tree.

"Dora, I have never admitted to you before, but I have done some baking in my life-time," Milton said when he heard of their predicament.

Dora's jaw dropped. "Will wonders ever cease?"

"I'm sure you are the better baker, but I could give it a go."

She kissed him on the top of his cropped red hair. "I'm willing to let you try. I have some tried-and- true recipes here on the table. The ingredients are already purchased. Pick out what you are willing to do, and I'll do my best to accommodate you."

Milton nodded and tied on one of Dora's full ruffled aprons. He perused the recipes she had chosen and selected the Russian teacakes. "I think I can handle this one."

"You're just too good for me, dear Milton." Dora turned her head, so he wouldn't see her laugh. She brought out the flour, butter, walnuts, and powdered sugar and set them on the counter and shared a few tips before she kissed him lightly and went out the door with Josie.

"Do you think Milton can bake?" Josie asked unconvinced.

Dora shrugged. "He continues to amaze me, and I really don't have any choice. I'm far too busy to be confined to the kitchen just now."

No one else was at the church to assist with the tree when they arrived. Denise had told Dora where to find the artificial tree and the decorations and apologized that she would not be there to help. The sisters hauled the tree out of the basement closet up the long flight of stairs to the front of the church. Luckily, the tree was of medium size even, but they struggled to bring it up the steep stairs. While Dora was fluffing out the branches, Josie went back to the closet for the decorations. "I don't remember these," Josie said as she pulled out religious themed ornaments.

Dora dug into the box. "They were purchased last year. Strange they didn't put these into a new box." The sisters wrapped the lights around the tree and then draped the silver garland. Then they added the ornaments. Dora reached in the bottom of the box and took out a small package and opened it, expecting to find additional hooks for ornaments. Instead, she brought out cardboard templates.

Dora's hand flew to her chest. "Josie, here are more of the Nativity templates."

"Can't be. Why are they found in different places? Wouldn't they be all together?"

Dora shuffled through them. "They should be."

"What are they?"

"The angels."

Josie peered over her shoulder. "Oh, I love angels. Let me see."

"It seems to me that different quilters did a certain part of the quilt on their own time."

"It would explain why all the templates aren't together in one place."

"Exactly."

"What figures are still missing?"

"I don't know for certain." Dora hesitated. "Baby Jesus and the manager for sure. Then there are the shepherds and the animals if they were included in the Nativity."

"I remember the Nativity story, but what if they included the scenes before it."

"For example?"

"The Angel appearing to Mary."

"And the Angel appearing to Joseph," Dora added. "I'll put these in my collection. I have been cutting them out of fabric to find out how they go together."

"What if you can't find all of them?"

"Then I'll improvise with another pattern."

Josie squinted. "And how are you going to complete another quilt. We don't even have the poinsettia quilt finished yet, and may I remind you it will be Alexia's wedding gift."

"I'm compelled to find out more about the Nativity quilt."

Josie wrinkled her brow. "It may not even be a quilt."

"I've thought of the possibility too, but it's highly probable it is a quilt."

Dora and Josie added the last two ornaments and uttered approval of their workmanship, unplugged the lights, and left the church.

It was late in the afternoon when they arrived home. Baked goodness filled the house with tantalizing odors. Immediately, Milton invited them into the kitchen. "I have hot water for tea and cookies," he sang out.

The sisters exchanged glances and whispered to one another that they smelled nothing burnt. Dora had expected to find the kitchen a disaster, but it appeared Milton did an admirable job of cleanup. The cookie's taste and texture would be the actual test, she thought. Milton poured the water into mugs and passed around the tea bags. With a flourish, he set a plate of cookies on the table. Neither sister wasted any time popping one into her mouth. "Yum," was Dora's response to the buttery and nutty goodness. "You're hired to do the rest of the holiday baking," she said with a wink.

Milton held up his hand. "Not so fast. I may have had one success, but that doesn't mean I'm to be entrusted with the rest."

Dora laughed. "How about being my assistant then?"

"I can do that. How did tree decorating go?" he asked.

Dora shared the details and told him about finding more templates. He lifted his brows in interest. "You have more to find?"

"We do," Josie said. "Isn't it strange the templates still exist after all these years?"

Dora stared out the window. "Odd, how they're waiting to be discovered."

———

After breakfast one morning, she talked Milton in taking her to the prairie church to retrieve the patterns she had left there. Josie stayed home to sew.

The drive to the church took only a few minutes. Dora searched for the key in her purse and opened the door. She immediately headed for the cupboard and removed the templates and handed them to Milton. "Here are more pieces to the puzzle. I want to cut these out of fabric and try to construct the quilt on my own even though it might not be the exact replica."

Milton picked up the cardboard figures. "What do you have here?"

"It's Mary and Joseph in different poses. Now all I have to determine is how they are used in the Nativity quilt."

Milton frowned. "Dora you're spreading yourself too thin. You don't even have one quilt done, and you're thinking of making another?"

She lowered her head. "I want to make this quilt. It's a mystery, a puzzle that desires to be completed. You should understand."

"In a way, I do. Where are the names Berta gave you? Have you done anything with them yet?"

"I haven't." She reached in her purse and pulled out a slip of paper. "The names don't mean a lot. I vaguely remember them as a child."

"A genealogy site or even an old church directory might help."

Dora squeezed his arm and smiled. "Are you offering your services?"

"I could help you out a little. Refresh my memory." He winked. "So far you have found the patterns in three different places?"

Dora nodded. "Yes, in my tote, the prairie church, and my church."

Milton pulled his phone from this pocket and brought up the picture of Dora's mother and the other women. "There are six women in this picture. You can identify all but one. Is that correct?"

"Yes."

"And you don't have all the patterns needed to complete a Nativity quilt?"

"Correct. Baby Jesus, the shepherds, and the animals are missing. There may be other figures I haven't considered."

"My guess is that each woman was entrusted with certain vignettes of the Nativity. If that's the case then there has to be at least three more pattern sets someplace, unless they were lost or destroyed."

Dora nodded. "Makes sense."

"We need to speak to the daughters of the women and see if someone remembers something about the Nativity quilt. Any ideas whom we start with?"

Dora studied the photograph again. She recognized Prudence Hanson. "I'm familiar with Mrs. Hanson's daughter, Violet. She lives in Hedge City, but she's in fragile health and is a resident in the rest home. I doubt if she would be helpful."

"Let's not assume, Dora. Anyone else in the picture?"

"Two of these ladies must have moved away. They are the ones on Berta's list. I don't remember them when I had grown up, but I know their names." She pointed to the woman next to the end. "This lady had no children and is deceased. I wouldn't know where to find someone to connect with her. And then there is this young woman who doesn't look familiar to me at all. My mother makes six. And I have found her part in the Nativity quilt which is the Wise Men."

"So for now, we have one lead."

"Not much to go on."

Milton stroked his chin. "I have solved cases with far less. Want to visit the rest home today?"

"I should get home and help Josie with the poinsettia quilt. I haven't done much."

Milton scratched his head. "Do you suppose the town's newspaper would have any information about a Nativity quilt?"

Dora brightened. "Sure, why didn't I think of that? A stop there wouldn't take too long."

"It's worth a try. Let's go check right now."

When she entered the newspaper office, Dora's eyes stung from the odor of fresh ink and newsprint. She wiped her eyes while they were directed to the stacks of old issues of the newspapers housed on shelves. To Dora's relief they weren't saved on microfilm. She disliked operating the fickle machine and squinting at the screen. After finding the newspapers for 1950, Milton and Dora began with December and worked backwards. She turned the brittle pages with extreme care. Luckily, church news occupied a corner of the weekly newspaper where Milton focused his attention. However, she paused occasionally to read a noteworthy event of which she remembered occurring during her youth. For a moment, she revisited her past and caught herself smiling in remembrance. Her recollections differed from the newspaper's account, but she was just a young girl then.

In one of the November papers, Milton found something noteworthy and let out a low whistle. Dora immediately turned her attention to him. Unfortunately, the report was comprised of a small paragraph in the church news explaining that several of the church ladies were in the final stages of a Nativity quilt to be displayed in the church on Christmas Eve. No names were given.

"A dead end," Dora complained.

"Not necessarily. At least we know for sure there was a Nativity quilt. We must find the church membership list for 1950 and scrutinize all the female members to see if we can find the identity of the woman in the picture."

"That will take time." Dora hesitated in thought. "Let's go home, so I can work on the quilt. Josie will become disgusted with me for always running out on her. We'll wait until tomorrow and visit the church. Hopefully, it won't be a dead end."

The days turned cold and occasionally snow spat against the windows. Dora and Josie feverishly worked on the quilt while Milton took over the baking with advice from Dora. Cinnamon spice and applesauce permeated the house when Milton volunteered to make the tree ornaments. He used the assortment of cookie cutters that Dora and Josie had accumulated over the years. The sisters took a break from their sewing to help him cut out the shapes of Christmas stockings, gingerbread men, stars, bells, houses, and teddy bears. Using a drinking straw, Milton made holes in which to insert ribbon to hang the cookies from the tree. For several hours while they were baking, the cinnamon aroma wafted through the house, tantalizing Milton into baking something edible.

"Since we have all the cookie cutters out, I will try my hand at molasses and ginger cookies," he told the ladies.

Dora clapped her hands. "Be our guest."

Dora and Josie returned to their sewing machines. Josie counted the completed quilt blocks and determined that over half the quilt blocks had been finished. She laid out the blocks on the Christmas print they had purchased and stood back for a look. "This print is perfect for the sashing. And then there is the quilting. Are we able to complete the quilting in time?"

Dora wound the bobbin. "I'm willing to pay someone to machine quilt for us. We don't have time to quilt it by hand."

"Good idea. I'll chip in half of the cost especially since the quilt will be Alexia's wedding gift."

"I hope someone has the time to quilt so close to Christmas."

Josie cut the thread on her completed block. "We'd better call someone soon."

Enticed by the aroma of molasses, cinnamon, and ginger, the ladies put their sewing aside and sneaked into the kitchen to sample Milton's cookies. Milton laughed when he saw them. "Just in time," he said as he placed a plate of delectable treats on the table.

"Don't forget cantata practice tonight," Milton reminded Dora.

"Let's go early, so we can look through directories and membership lists."

Josie brushed crumbs from her lips. "What are you looking for?"

"The identity of the woman in the picture," Dora said. "Why weren't we aware of her when we were growing up?"

Josie shook her head. "Where do you suppose she came from if she wasn't from Hedge City?"

"You have a point. She may not have been from here. Did your pastor preach in additional churches?" Milton asked.

"Why yes. There used to be a small community named Rock Falls about fifteen miles from here. Nothing much is there anymore."

Josie reached for another cookie. "I've heard there are a few residents still living there."

"We'll see tonight if we can come up with a name in the church records," Milton said. "If we can't, we might investigate this ghost town."

In the evening, Milton and Dora left Josie home sewing. They arrived at church forty minutes before cantata practice. Fortunately, Dora knew where to find the directories and the membership rolls. Milton wasn't familiar with any names, requiring her to do the searching. She flipped through the pages and began in the late 1940s. Most of the names she recognized as part of the community, but there were a few she jotted down on paper. It had been years since she had been through these records, but she noted a volume she hadn't seen before. Brushing the dust off its cover, she opened it to discover the membership roll for the church in Rock Falls which had been served by pastors of her church. The names were mostly foreign to her, although she copied the roll for 1950 in hopes someone could make a connection between the woman in the picture and the name.

Before cantata practice, Dora approached several older women with the list of names. They apologized that they weren't able to give her any more leads. Dora hung her head in defeat and thanked them, anyway.

"I keep coming to a dead end," she complained to Milton.

"We still have Violet at the rest home and a visit to the abandoned town. Maybe we'll get a break then."

Dora scowled at his optimism and joined the altos in song.

After cantata practice, they left immediately and found Josie asleep on the sofa. "Poor dear wore herself out sewing." Dora draped an afghan over her and met Milton in the kitchen where they strung green and red ribbon through the holes in the cinnamon ornaments. "We'll wait until tomorrow, so Josie can help us hang them on the tree."

Milton held up an ornament and sneezed. "The entire house smells of cinnamon."

Dora laughed. "Hope you aren't allergic."

―――

The next day after breakfast, Milton went outside to tinker with his light display. Josie walked over to Julia's with the promise she would be back to accompany Dora to the quilters guild meeting. Dora was left to sew until then. She worked a while on the poinsettia quilt, but the Nativity templates drew her from the sewing machine to the box where she stored them. Eager to see what the angels would look in white fabric, she opened the doors of her sewing cupboard and pulled out a lustrous remnant of white material. Carefully tracing around the pattern, she cut out several angels, thinking about the host of angels described in the Bible. Satisfied she had enough for now, she scrutinized Mary and Joseph who appeared in several poses. A beige fabric seemed appropriate for Joseph, and she selected a light shade of blue for Mary. They would appear in all scenes dressed in the same colors. She opened the Bible to Luke and Matthew to reacquaint herself with the Christmas story.

Dora read that the angel Gabriel had appeared to Mary revealing to her she would give birth to God's son. Gabriel also visited Joseph and told him not to be afraid. His finance was pure, and it was God plan for her to give birth to a savior.

These biblical events held a pertinent place in the Nativity quilt. The original quilt must have included these events, she thought. The quilt formed in her mind, but the one nagging question was how she would be able to complete the quilt in time for Christmas.

Josie stopped by around ten to take her to the quilting guild. "I'm anxious to see how plans are progressing," Dora confided to Josie on the way to the meeting.

Dora had relinquished her job as president to Faye several years ago when they left on their retirement trips. No longer an officer, she sat back and listened. So far a dozen antique quilts had been entered in the Christmas quilt show and at least another dozen newly crafted Christmas quilts were being made. The number of unique Christmas trees to be displayed were yet unknown. Dora thought about Milton and her idea for trees made from old doors. She wondered how long it would take him to make one and if he had the tools to do so.

Faye opened the meeting up to a discussion of Christmas quilts and the various patterns and ideas that were being used. The range of possibilities seemed endless. Josie brought a block from their poinsettia quilt to share with the quilters. The discussion generated many ideas.

Toward the end of the conversation, Dora shared her discovery of the Nativity quilt. Dora told them how and where she found the templates and the newspaper report verifying its existence. No one at the meeting had ever heard of a Nativity quilt made in their community. "I only have three or perhaps four more sets to find," she explained. "If anyone has an idea where they might be, please let me know."

The members seemed interested, and Dora explained she thought it would be a grand gesture to make the quilt as a guild project. "I don't have time to complete it myself. Would anyone be interested in appliquéing the patterns?" she asked.

"Ordinarily we would love to," someone said. "But we have our own quilts to finish and time is fleeting fast."

"I know I'm imposing on your time. But I thought if everyone did a small part, the quilt could be finished in time to display. I have pieces cut out already. The ones we can't find will be replicated from other patterns. Think about it over lunch," she suggested.

Several people who hadn't planned a complicated quilt project came up to Dora during lunch and volunteered to help. "We'll get together shortly to determine the fabric for the background and the layout," Dora said, beaming with the interest.

On their way home, Josie turned to Dora and commented in surprise. "I had no idea you would propose another quilt idea to the guild. Aren't we all going to be over extended?"

"We may be, but we will be blessed."

———

Alexia pounded on Dora's door early the next morning as if there was an emergency. Dora, though in her housecoat, opened the door to her frantic niece. "Oh, Dora, I don't know what to do. My daycare help all came down with the flu, and I'm alone. Do you think you and Josie could help me out today?"

Dora pulled her robe close around her. "Us? You want us to help take care of children?"

"Yes, I'll be there. I need someone to help keep order and assist with snack time and lunch. Read a story and sing. Please, I'm desperate," Alexia pleaded.

Josie heard the last of the conversation and smiled at the suggestion. "Come on Dora. It might be fun. As long as Alexia is there to supervise, we should be able to handle a few kids."

Dora rolled her eyes and agreed. "It's against my better judgment. When do you want us there?"

"In an hour. Thanks. Love you both." Alexia closed the door and fled.

"When are we going to finish the quilt?" Dora asked Josie. "Something always interrupts our plans."

"Have faith it will get done even if we have to burn the proverbial midnight oil. Now hurry and get dressed. We have a job to do."

The ladies dressed in record time and got to the daycare after all the children had arrived. Alexia was doing her best to settle the children into the routine. Several three-year-olds were crying, and Josie tried to calm them, but they didn't cease until Alexia took them by the hand and lead them to a play center.

Dora wrung her hands. "What do you want me to do?"

"They probably feel insecure with strangers. Just be friendly and smile Dora."

She faked a smile and circulated through the room doing her best to be friendly and helpful. Josie had already convinced the children to call her grandma. The morning passed with a few incidents. Alexia took care of them with deft skill while Dora and Josie looked on.

Lunch proved to be messy with more macaroni and cheese under the table than was eaten. Once the children were cleaned up, from the cheesy goop, they were bedded down on rugs for nap time. A soothing video played in the background lulling most to sleep.

Both Dora and Josie plopped in chairs to rest. Alexia straightened up the room and joined them for a brief respite. "You ladies are amazing. I'm so thankful you volunteered to help me out."

"Will you have help tomorrow?" Dora asked, lifting her brow.

"I have two young girls coming in tomorrow. You'll be off the hook."

Josie lowered her voice. "How are wedding plans coming?"

"I've been busy here. Mother is doing a good job. It's just the reception we're worrying about and my wedding dress. If I'm to wear Mother's I'll need alterations."

"Bring it by tomorrow after work, and we'll see what has to be done."

Most of the children took an hour nap. They felt refreshed, but Dora and Josie were dragging. The afternoon proved to be the most challenging with tantrums and fatigue. The sisters read stories, but the children became inattentive.

Even though it wasn't on the schedule, Alexia brought out the play dough which entertained them until five o'clock when most of the working mothers picked up their children. After gathering up play dough fragments, Dora and Josie left for home, stopped at a restaurant for takeout, and spent the rest of the evening in easy-chairs. Neither one wanted to sew.

———

Several days later in the late afternoon, Alexia came by with her mother's wedding dress. Both Dora and Josie had sewed all day and the living room was strewn with fabric scraps amid the completed blocks. Josie spotted Alexia coming up the walk. "Here comes Alexia with the wedding dress. Hide the quilt."

"She'll see it at the quilt show," Dora reminded her. "Remember she won't know it will be her wedding present."

"Oh, sure. I nearly forgot."

Dora met her at the door and took the lace dress from her and invited her for a cup of tea. "How was your day?"

"A rat race. I was short one helper today, but we made it through. If you don't mind, Aunt Dora, set the entire pot of tea on the table." Dora did as she wished. Josie dipped in the cookie jar and filled a plate.

"I hope the alterations won't become a challenge. If it does, I'll just buy a new one."

"You have tried it on?" Josie asked.

Alexia sat down wearily. "I have. It must to be taken in a little. I'm no seamstress, but it shouldn't be too difficult." She dipped a cookie in the tea. "I'd like to involve both of you in the wedding."

"We'd be honored." Dora spoke for them both. "What did you have in mind?"

"How about cutting the cake? I've ordered it from Lana Duncan. She's well known for her wedding cakes."

Josie smiled. "We'd be delighted. I love weddings."

Alexia glanced at her watch. "It's getting late. Are you ready for the alterations?"

"We are. Use my bedroom and slip the dress on," Dora said.

"We'll need to shop for new outfits, too," Josie whispered to Dora. "We can't appear dowdy cutting the cake."

"I was thinking about wearing my wedding dress. I mean the bridesmaid dress I wore to yours," Dora said.

Josie ran her fingers through her golden hair. "I for one want something new."

In a few minutes, Alexia hummed the wedding march as she entered the living room. Josie gasped. "Alexia, you are beautiful. I forgot how lovely Julia's dress was."

"Please zip me up," Alexia said while straining with the zipper. "I can't reach it."

Josie accommodated her and accomplished the zipping with a little tugging. "It's difficult to get past the bodice and the full skirt. I like how it billows out similar to a fairy princess dressed in the finest lace. The sleeves are long and modest unlike the wedding dresses of today."

Alexia shivered. "A strapless would be too cold for this time of year."

"Where's the veil?" Dora suddenly noticed Alexia wasn't wearing it.

"I left it at home. It's in fine shape."

"If I remember right, it's held by a small pearl crown?"

"It is."

"And what will you wear for jewelry?"

"Mother's pearls. They are the real thing."

"Goode choice," Josie said. The aunts buzzed around Alexia, pulling and pinning at the same time.

"Just a few tucks here and there and the dress will fit perfectly," Dora said with pins clinched between her teeth.

"Wonderful. I really didn't want to buy a new dress. I adore the patina of the old lace although it has yellowed some."

"All the more beautiful." Josie scrutinized the street length dress finished with scalloped edges. "What type of flowers did you choose for your bouquet?"

"Something red and white for Christmas. I'm not sure what yet?"

"I'm so excited," Josie gushed. "And the bridesmaids. What will they wear?"

"Silver and red. We haven't shopped for dresses yet."

Dora added the last pin. "You had better get to it. No doubt they will have to be ordered. Now, carefully slip out of the dress. We should be done with it in a few days."

After Alexia changed, she kissed her aunts goodbye and promised she'd update them as to plans and left for home.

Josie set the dress aside. "I for one am looking forward to her old fashioned wedding just like the traditional Christmas we have planned. We'll just pretend we have stepped back in time."

Dora shook her head. "I'm not sure we can step back in time no matter how hard we try."

"The whereabouts of the rest of the Nativity templates is driving me crazy," Dora burst out while she was sewing the next morning.

Josie finished taking in the seams on Alexia's wedding dress. She turned toward her and scowled. "Where else can you look?"

"I don't know. The women who volunteered to help with the quilt need the patterns to work with." Dora tossed her the tape measure. "Milton and I have done a genealogy search for the two women who moved away and have found nothing encouraging. Violet may have something, but I doubt it. She's been a resident at the rest home for several years. The unidentified lady might have something. But where is she? I'm drawing a blank."

"Why are you obsessed with this quilt? Frankly it's getting on my nerves."

"It would add so much to the prairie church. Alexia could use it as a focal point in her wedding."

"What makes you think Alexia wants a Nativity quilt in her wedding?"

"I envision the quilt to be beautiful and reflective of the season."

"I'm sure it will be. But I believe Alexia has other plans." Josie paused and glanced at her sister. "In fact, when we complete the poinsettia quilt, I plan on returning home for a while before Christmas. I miss Anthony."

Dora paled. "You won't be here to work on the Nativity quilt?"

"Sorry, but I have things to do at home before we come back for Christmas. Originally, I thought we'd have a quiet time

60

together while working on the annual Christmas quilt. However, you are distracted to the point of worry."

A pained expression crossed her face. "I'm sorry, too. I didn't intend for so much to be happening in such a short time. How many days until we finish the quilt?"

"Only four blocks to go and then we'll sew on the sashing. I'd say about four days tops."

"How do you plan on getting back to Iowa?"

"The bus. I've talked to Anthony, and he wants me home, too."

"Can't say I blame you. Sorry I've been a pain."

"We've got on each other's nerves before. Not to worry. Now, back to your dilemma."

"Oh, yes. Where to find the patterns."

"You're assuming that only the women in the photo made the quilt. What if there was someone else, but she wasn't photographed that day?"

"You're right, but who could that be?"

"We've never considered the minister's wife in 1950."

"Who was it?"

"I don't know, but there must be a record somewhere that would tell us."

Dora frowned. "She's probably deceased, too."

"Perhaps, although she may have a daughter who was a quilter."

"So that means another trip to the church's archives."

Josie peered in the mirror and fluffed her warm blonde hair. "Let's drop this dress off for Alexia and then visit the church. Maybe Julia can brew us a cup of coffee while we're there."

Alexia wasn't home to try on the dress, but Josie left instructions to call them if it still didn't fit. They lingered over coffee with Julia while she rattled on about the wedding. "We went shopping for bridesmaid dresses the other day. Alexia couldn't find what she was looking for."

"What's she going to do?" Josie asked.

"I don't know. I asked her but she seemed discouraged. She's working too hard at the daycare and doesn't have enough time to focus on her wedding." Julia paused. "Would you two be able to sew the bridesmaids' dresses if we need you to?"

Dora sat speechless, and Josie blurted out quickly she had planned to go home to Iowa. Anthony was missing her.

Julia flushed. "I'm being presumptuous."

Dora found her voice and forced a question. "How many attendants are you talking about?"

"Two women and two men. Alexia sees no need for six bridesmaids."

"I agree. I suppose two dresses wouldn't be difficult," Dora said halfheartedly while thinking about her Nativity quilt.

"I'm uncertain the dresses will have to be made, but time is running short on ordering any." Julia turned toward Josie. "Don't change your plans on our account. I understand."

"I'm sorry to leave you gals, but I need to return home a while."

"Do I know the bridesmaids?" Dora asked.

"I believe you know Diane from church."

"Yes, I had her in school. And the other?"

"Jennie."

Josie's face brightened. "She is one of my best library patrons."

Dora rose from the table. "Josie and I are on an errand. We must get going. Keep us posted."

"When are you leaving, Josie?" Julia asked.

"In a few days."

Julia hugged her and wished her well. "See you on Christmas."

Dora drove to the church and let them in using a pass code. In the library, they searched through the archives and found the name of the minister and his wife who served during the 1950s. Pastor Joshua Helms and his wife Sandra were listed as serving in the church for several years. However, no other specifics were given.

"We have their names but nothing else," Josie commented.

"Maybe Violet will know something more. I must ask her when we go to the rest home the next time."

Dora became more and more anxious as the days progressed to find the rest of the Nativity quilt templates. She asked Milton if he would accompany her to see Violet in the rest home. Violet was just a few years older than she but had many physical challenges in the past few years. As far as Dora knew, Violet still had a sharp mind.

Violet knew who Dora was when she knocked on her open door and came into the room. They reminisced briefly about attending the same school and church. Violet had lived on the other side of town, and since she was ahead of Dora in school, they hadn't become fast friends.

Dora explained the Nativity quilt to Violet and admitted that she knew nothing about it but had found some templates in her mother's things. She asked Violet if she knew anything about such a quilt.

Violet was about to shake her head when Dora showed her the picture of the six ladies who she thought were the quilt's crafters. "Can you identify these ladies?" she asked.

Violet looked closely and smiled, pointing to her mother. "And here's your mother," she said. She identified the other women also but stopped momentarily at the unidentified lady.

"Do you know her?" Dora prompted.

Violet squinted. "She looks familiar. I'm trying to come up with her name."

"She may be from another town other than Hedge City."

"You don't know who she is?"

Dora opened the roll book from Rock Falls and unfolded her list from the church record of names she was not familiar with. "No one I have asked knows the unidentified woman's name, but I'll read off a list of names. See if any name is familiar to you." Dora read quite a few names until Violet stopped her.

"Read that last name again."

"Ellen Good."

"Yes, I believe that is the name of the woman in the photograph."

Dora's heart skipped a beat. "Who was she?"

"She was from another town. In fact, I think it was Rock Falls. I vaguely remember her. She came by our house a few times to work on a quilt. Perhaps it was your Nativity quilt."

"Could it be?" Dora's eyes sparkled. "Are you sure you don't remember any details about the quilt?"

Violet closed her eyes in thought. Dora remained silent, waiting. "I seem to recall angels. In fact, my mother let me play with a couple. I liked to put them in the branches of the Christmas tree. Yes, it could have been the Nativity quilt."

"Do you remember anything more?"

Violet shook her head.

Dora glanced at Milton who was seated beside her. He hadn't said anything since they arrived. "I know where Rock Falls used to be but there's not much left of the town, anymore. Do you know if Ellen had any children?" she asked Violet.

"I can't answer that question." Violet pulled at her sweat shirt. "Like I said I barely knew her."

"Do you remember your mother having any patterns for a Nativity quilt?"

"No, but it's likely Ellen and my mother were working together. Ellen may have had the patterns."

Dora pursed her lips. "It's possible Ellen may still be alive."

Violet nodded. "It's possible. In the picture she looks to be younger than the other women."

"I have another name for you. In fact, it's the former minister Joshua Helms and his wife Sandra. Do you remember them?"

"Briefly. I was young then."

"According to the church records they were only here for a short time. Would you happen to know where they went after leaving Hedge City?"

"I don't know, but my mother was good about writing such things down. She didn't keep a diary; however, she jotted events down in a notebook."

Dora slid to the edge of her chair. "Do you have the notebook?"

"I forgot about it until we talked. There might be something in it to help you."

"Do you have it here with you?"

"Open the bottom drawer of the dresser," Violet directed. "It's blue and falling apart. I only keep it because it's my mom's handwriting."

Dora's hands shook as she sorted through the drawer's contents until she found the book. She handed it to Violet.

Violet turned the pages haphazardly. "Mother didn't organize her notes well. They're random, but at least she scrawled in the dates."

"Could you begin in 1950?"

Violet fumbled with the notebook and finally handed it to Dora. "There's nothing personal in here, so you might as well do the looking."

Violet was right. Short notes were written hurriedly sometimes in pencil, other times in ink. A date was usually included and often even the month was penned into the margins. After a time, she found entries for 1950. Violet's mother mentioned quilting meetings, but didn't describe what they were quilting, but she noted Ellen Good's name. To Dora's disappointment no mention was made of a Nativity quilt. She flipped through the rest of the decade.

Dora thanked Violet for the information and promised to let her know if she found any more regarding the quilt. She also made a mental note to bring her a Christmas basket. She shuddered at the lonely life Violet led. It could have been her in failing health and relegated to a rest home, but she had a family, Milton, her sisters, and Anthony. How thankful she was for them.

On the way home, Milton discussed the new information with Dora.

"It's unlikely Ellen is living in Rock Falls," Dora said. "Surely, she would have made an appearance in Hedge City at some time or another."

"We should look, anyway. There might be someone there who knows or knew of her. I'll drive you there tomorrow."

The trip to Rock Falls turned cloudy and threatened snow. Within a half hour they came to a place where Rock Falls once flourished. Now, only a few dilapidated buildings were the only evidence of a town. Milton drove through what appeared to be Main Street and then branched off on a few trails which had once been side streets. Curling smoke from a chimney led them to a small house hidden by leafless trees.

Dora peered from the car window. "Rather forlorn."

"Did you want to stop and inquire?"

"I... I don't know. I suppose I should. Do you think anyone is home?"

"The smoke coming out of the chimney would say so."

Dora sat motionless. "Yes, you're probably right."

"You want me to go with you?"

"Would you?"

"There's nothing to fear."

Milton parked near the house in a bad state of repair. The smell of wood smoke was the only assurance someone inhabited the house. Milton rapped on the door. No one answered. He rapped again and waited. Dora shrugged and turned from the door when a thin, wrinkled woman's face emerged from the doorway.

Uncharacteristically, Milton groped for words. "I'm Milton and this is my wife Dora. We... we're looking for a woman by the name of Ellen Good."

She eyed them cautiously. "What for?"

"Ah, I..." Milton glanced to Dora for help.

Dora cleared her throat and spoke rather rapidly. "I'm researching a Nativity quilt that was made in the 1950s. My mother Bea helped with the quilt. Unfortunately, I was too young to remember anything about it. I was told you might be one of the crafters." Dora pulled out the picture of the six quilters from her purse and handed it to Ellen.

The woman studied the photograph for a while. Dora was about to give up hope. "I'm the youngest one of the group," the woman said. "I'm Ellen Good."

Dora clutched her chest. "I... I would like to visit with you. You see, I have found some templates for that quilt but some are missing, and I would like to find them."

"Why?"

Dora shuffled her feet. "I know it might sound strange, but I would like to make that quilt again, with help."

Ellen's gray eyes inspected the couple carefully. "You are Bea's daughter. You look a little like her." Ellen opened the door wider. "Come in."

Dora exhaled and smiled slightly as she entered a dark room. "Do you live here by yourself?" She asked while scrutinizing the bleak kitchen.

Ellen snapped on the kitchen light. "Most of the time."

Dora wrinkled her brow and glanced at Milton. She wanted to know what Ellen meant by the response, but Milton shook his head.

"I live in Hedge City, but I haven't seen you there," Dora said.

"Oh, I never go to Hedge City."

"You must get supplies somewhere?" she insisted.

Ellen sat down at the table. "I usually have someone bring me what I need."

Dora waited until Ellen seated herself at the table and then joined her. "Could you tell me about the Nativity quilt?"

"We made a Nativity quilt, but it was long ago. The women you see in the photo are the ones who made it."

"No one else helped?"

"No, just the women pictured."

Ellen's response ruled out Sandra Helms, Dora thought.

"Why do you ask?"

"Oddly, I have found quilt templates, but some are still missing. I realize it's been a long time ago, and the rest of the patterns could have been thrown away." Dora hesitated. "I can't seem to give up hope of finding them. Can you help?"

Ellen's eyes narrowed. "In what way?"

"Do you have any of the Nativity templates?"

"I have kept all my quilting patterns. They are in several boxes." Ellen motioned toward a closet. "You want me to look, now?"

"If you don't mind. Time is fleeting, and I was hoping to finish the Nativity quilt before Christmas."

Ellen limped to the closet and lifted out a box. While she sorted through her patterns, Dora asked more questions.

"What was special about the Nativity quilt?"

"It was made as a going away gift for our Pastor Joshua Helms and his wife Sandra."

"Strange, as I was going to try to find Sandra Helms and see if she was one of the quilters."

"She wasn't and didn't know about the surprise. She thought we made it for the church. We displayed it for a while and then gave it to them."

"Do you know if the couple is still living?"

"I don't know."

Dora watched as Ellen dug deeper in the box in hopes she would pull out the rest of the missing templates. "What part of the quilt did you do? I've determined everyone was assigned to a certain segment."

Ellen sat with a stack of templates in her hand. "What patterns do you have?"

"I have the Wise Men, the angels, and Mary and Joseph."

Ellen held up several patterns. "I was assigned the shepherds and the sheep."

Dora stared at the templates before her. "It's a miracle. I found the Wise Men with our sewing things. My mother probably appliquéd that scene." Suddenly Dora had a thought. "Then you know you made all the other figures on the quilt?"

Ellen handed the shepherds and sheep to Dora.

She reached for them as if they would break and turned each one over and over in her hand. "I can't believe these patterns have still survived. Now if only I could find them all. Let me ask you again. Do you know who made the other parts of the quilt?"

"Tell me where you found the other templates."

"I found Mary and Joseph at the prairie church."

"Yes, we met at the church where we appliquéd the quilt. We kept our patterns in the cupboard when they weren't needed," Ellen explained.

"I found the angels at the church in town. That leaves perhaps more animals and the most important part of the Nativity, Jesus. Do you know where he is?"

"You ask a profound question," Ellen said with a demure smile. "To the believer, he's in our hearts. God's lost sheep are the unbelievers. They don't have Jesus in their hearts."

Ellen didn't answer the question she had asked, but Dora suddenly realized the purpose of her mission to find the Nativity quilt. She was searching for Jesus not unlike the shepherds or the Wise Men or the world that needed a Savior. She had been on a mission of finding a pattern but discovered, instead, a need to establish a deeper relationship with her Savior. She had always been a believer, but had she matured in her faith? Had she really worked at becoming Christ like? Had she always been too preoccupied with her own needs and wants?

The revelation Ellen pointed out to her left her weak and ashamed, but at the same time a burning fire of discovery ignited within her. She glanced at Milton to see if he felt the same. He smiled at her. Yes, she thought. He understands. Who was this woman who had opened her eyes?

———

Members of the church met the next day to fill baskets with fruit, nuts, and candies for the shut-ins and the elderly. Dora had helped with this project in the past; however, this time she had names of people to put on the list. There were dear Violet in the rest home and Ellen Good who lived a remote life, seemingly alone most of the time. She had more questions to ask of her.

Dora mentioned Ellen's name to the group, but no one knew her and was surprised to learn she had lived in Hedge City once. There was a mystery about this woman. Dora was willing to investigate.

After the members filled the baskets, they split the task of delivering them. Dora volunteered to distribute Berta, Violet, and Ellen's baskets. Milton was busy helping set up the Nativity scene in front of the church, so Dora went alone. She stopped at the rest home first where she found Violet sitting in a chair by her bed. Dora placed the basket on a small table much to

Violet's delight. Dora removed the cellophane, so Violet could sample the contents.

During their conversation, Dora asked Violet if she remembered anymore about the Nativity quilt. Violet nodded and motioned for her to retrieve the blue notebook from her chest of drawers.

"The other day I leafed through my mother's journal to see if I could find more information for you. My memory has been fading lately, and I don't remember as I used to."

"I have that problem, too." Dora smiled.

"I forgot that Mom entered several comments about Ellen Good. They must have gotten acquainted when they worked on the quilt." Violet opened to a passage she had bookmarked. "Here, read this."

Dora read the brief entry. 'Ellen didn't show up for quilting today. I hope the town is proud of itself." Dora dropped the notebook in her lap. "What does this mean?"

"I don't know. Now that I think about it, Ellen did disappear."

Dora didn't remain long in Violet's room. Violet became tired, and a nurse helped her back in bed. Dora promised to come by for another visit and left to stop by Berta's room with a basket. Berta was asleep but awoke when Dora entered. "What have you got," she asked Dora weakly.

"A Christmas basket of fruit, nuts, and candy."

"Thank you. Put it on my table." She pushed a button and raised herself in order to see Dora better. "You were just by to see me the other day. Something about a quilt?"

Dora nodded. "The Nativity quilt."

"Did you find what you were looking for?"

"Not yet. Still searching." Dora noticed that Berta was eyeing the basket. "Would you like me to core an apple for you?"

"I would. I can still chew," Berta said laughing.

"I was wondering if you knew a lady by the name of Ellen Good?"

"The name sounds familiar, but I can't say I knew her."

"She lived in Hedge City but was said to have disappeared."

"Oh, let me think. I seem to remember something about a disappearing young woman."

"Do you remember why she disappeared?"

"No. I never paid attention to gossip."

Dora cut Berta's apple into quarters and bid her goodbye. She was most anxious to see Ellen again.

She hoped Ellen would be home although she doubted she ever went anywhere. Another woman living a lonely life, she thought to herself. Within a half-an-hour she pulled up to the little house hidden by trees. Taking the basket, she picked her way through the icy snow to the house. Ellen must have heard her car for she opened the door immediately.

Dora handed her the basket. A smile emerged in the wrinkled face. "Come in. I was hoping you would come back."

"We haven't finished our conversation, and besides I wanted to bring you Christmas cheer."

Ellen filled her teakettle with water and placed it on the burner to heat. She sat down and waited for Dora to begin the conversation.

"I'm still wondering where to look for the missing pieces of the quilt. I was expecting you to tell me who made portions of the quilt and where I might find the templates. But you didn't."

"I don't know where the missing pieces to the quilt are." Ellen ran her fingers through her disheveled hair. "I know Violet's mother, Prudence, took over the rest of the quilt. The two ladies in the photograph who moved away were responsible for the animals and the stable. They had trouble with the appliqué, so Prudence helped them. Prudence finished with Jesus and the manger."

"You don't have those missing pieces?"

"No, I don't. I left everything other than the shepherds and sheep with Prudence."

Dora fingered her necklace. "I asked Violet about this, and she had no information or templates."

"I'm not surprised. Violet is about your age. Like you, she wouldn't remember."

"I asked her about her mother's mementoes, but Violet only has her mother's facsimile of a diary. The Nativity quilt is not mentioned." Dora paused. "She mentions you."

Ellen flushed. "What does she say?"

Dora's heart fluttered. "That you disappeared."

Ellen didn't comment. She poured the tea and changed the subject. Dora wanted to ask her why she disappeared but couldn't bring herself to interfere in her life. Seeing that Ellen didn't want to talk, anymore, Dora left shortly and returned to the rest home to see Violet again.

Luckily, she wasn't sleeping. "Sorry to disturb you again, Violet, but I have another question for you."

Violet rubbed her eyes. "I'll try my best to answer you."

"Ellen Good told me that your mom, Prudence, had the last of the Nativity templates."

"She might have, but the contents of her house were auctioned off last year."

"I probably wasn't here," Dora said, realizing she was traveling. Oh darn, Dora thought, the templates are gone forever.

"Don't fret. My mom wasn't a saver. No doubt she destroyed the templates as soon as the quilt was finished."

Dora's heart fell. She had come to the end of the road.

Dora was too disappointed to share with Milton she had to admit defeat in finding the rest of the Nativity quilt patterns, but Milton knew something was wrong. "Tell me Dora what's troubling you," he asked her at lunch the next day. "You've been moping around the house all morning."

"Oh, Milton, I can't locate the rest of the patterns I need to make the Nativity quilt."

"Why do you say that? I've never known you to quit."

"I have to let go of my idea. I found out from Ellen Good that Prudence Hanson had the rest of the patterns in her possession. Violet doesn't have them and doesn't remember where they could have been. While Josie and I were gone, Prudence's things were auctioned off." Dora frowned. "Besides, Violet told me that her mother wasn't a saver and that the patterns were probably discarded after the quilt was finished."

Milton nodded. "I see what you mean. What are you missing?"

"Ellen had the shepherds and sheep, so that leaves only Jesus and the manager."

"Then what's the problem? Either find a pattern or draw out one yourself. It may not be the original, but you will complete the quilt."

Dora knitted her brows. "I could."

"Besides, without the original quilt, you won't know how it was laid out and put together. The message it conveys will be the same."

"You're right. It was a silly idea of replicating the original. The guild and I will make up our own quilt. In fact, I'll work on finding a pattern after I do the dishes."

He patted her on the shoulder. "That a girl. I'm off to help set up the risers for the last cantata practice."

"I hope no one faints. I've seen it happen too many times."

Milton gestured thumbs up and kissed her goodbye.

Dora hurried through dishes and then settled in her chair with a stack of quilting books and her iPad. She found several figures of baby Jesus that might work. Taking the cardboard patterns of Mary and Joseph, she compared their size to that of baby Jesus. She selected the one that would work best. There were several versions of the stable which she drew out for the guild ladies to decide. Satisfied that she finally accepted the quilt as it was to be, she called Faye and told her she had all the pieces and was ready to meet with the ladies and begin the project.

———

The house seemed too quiet now that Josie left for Iowa but not before she and Dora worked long hours to finish the poinsettia quilt top. Dora had found someone to machine quilt it before the quilt show. When Dora sighed with relief that another project had been completed, Alexia called in panic once again. "I don't want to put you out, Aunt Dora, but I was wondering if you could sew my bridesmaid's dresses." Dora groaned, but how could Dora refuse her only niece? Her meeting with the guild ladies would have to wait.

Julia offered to help with the dresses, but Dora was skeptical of what she could do. She had never been interested in sewing like Dora and Josie had.

Julia, Alexia, and her bridesmaids, Diane and Jennie, were to arrive around nine that morning. Dora hurriedly cleaned up the kitchen and waited in the dining room with a pot of coffee and fresh baked lemon poppy seed muffins. Milton escaped to the garage.

Julia didn't bother to knock and once inside the door apologized for being late. Alexia and the young women carried in fabric, trim, and what looked like patterns. Dora hadn't been invited to choose either material or design and was hoping it would be simple enough to complete in a few days. She invited them to muffins and a cup of coffee before they discussed patterns.

Dora was surprised to see how Diane had blossomed these past few years. She remembered her as a shy teenager with little ambition. Jennie was as vivacious as Alexia. Dora smiled at their youth.

Over muffins, Julia and Alexia discussed the wedding plans completed so far. Invitations had been sent out, the wedding dress had been altered and sent to the cleaners, the minister had been commissioned, an organist found, tuxedos rented, flowers and wedding cake ordered. Pots and pots of poinsettias had been purchased at the local discount store. Everything had been done except securing a venue for the wedding reception and finding the bridesmaid dresses.

"Do you think we should have a Christmas tree at the church for our wedding?" Alexia asked Dora.

Dora grimaced, feeling she was put on the spot. "What do the rest of you think?"

"We're somewhat divided on the idea," her niece said. "Red and white poinsettias will take center stage at the church along with greenery and soft light. I love Christmas trees but again it might take up too much space."

"I agree with you," Dora said. "How about a Christmas tree at the reception, instead?"

"I like that idea except I don't even know where the reception will be."

"Table the decision for now. Show me your dress ideas."

Alexia spread patterns featuring different dress styles and fabric samples before her aunt. "I bought swatches of red and silver fabric that I like. I believe I have narrowed it down, but I want to see what you think."

Dora perused the patterns before her. She sighed with gratefulness that none were strapless or long gowns. Alexia had chosen street length dresses with fitted bodices. The only differences were the skirts. One was full and the other straight. At the moment she wished, Josie, her fashion conscious sister was here to help her decide. "Since your gown has been made with a fitted bodice and full skirt, I would think the bridesmaids' dresses should mimic the same." She lifted her brows and waited for the answer.

Alexia clapped her hands. "I totally agree, although I'm not sure how to combine the silver and red."

Diane spoke. "I was thinking of a silver bodice and red skirt, silver shoes and jewelry."

Dora winced. "We don't want to outshine the bride."

Alexia frowned. "What would you suggest?"

"I'm not the expert here," Dora said. "Julia help me out."

"Dora may be right. Alexia, your dress is antique white. You will carry red and white flowers. Instead of silver, I suggest antique white as the complementary color to red?"

Diane and Jennie looked at each other and nodded. Alexia screwed up her face and held her breath. "You may be right. I'll concede the silver and shop for antique lace."

Dora nodded and smiled. "Let's see about sizes for you gals." She removed a tape measure from her sewing kit and measured the young women. Diane wore a size seven and Jennie a size ten. Dora turned over the pattern and checked for construction and yardage. "Great. I see no problem here. As soon as you bring me the fabric, I'll begin. I hope to call you in for fittings in one week."

Alexia pecked her on the cheek. "Aunt Dora, you are amazing."

At the moment, Dora didn't feel amazing. Did she say one week?

———

Alexia had made an appointment to meet with Lana Duncan the wedding cake baker. She invited Julia and Dora to come along. That morning Julia had been over to Dora's cutting out the bridesmaids' dresses. Using the dining room table as a cutting surface, Dora laid out the patterns on the material Alexia had purchased. She checked the directions several times to avoid error and placed a few pins to hold the tissue patterns in place. Julia added more pins and cut around each piece. When Julia finished the cutting, Dora sewed the cut pieces together. The sisters had made considerable progress in the two hours before Alexia picked them up. "Could I see what you have done?" she asked when she found them busy in the living room.

"Sure, but it'll be hard to envision the finished product with just a few pieces sewn," Dora warned her.

Alexia held up the bodice partially completed. "I like the antique white. It's so traditional looking. You were right to talk me out of the silver."

The ladies placed the sewing project aside to concentrate on the wedding cake. "Do you have any ideas?" Dora asked Alexia.

"I'm not sure. Do I want something modern, or do I want something more traditional?"

Julia smiled. "That's your decision, daughter dear. Lana will have ideas."

"Even though Lana has lived in the same town as we have for a few years, I don't' really know her," Dora commented. "She doesn't attend our church, but she quilts although we haven't been in the same quilting groups."

"But she makes beautiful cakes," Julia pointed out. "In fact she's won awards for her cakes. She doesn't talk about herself very much."

"Does she have a family?" Dora asked.

"I don't believe so. Her husband died, and she never remarried."

"I don't recall any of her children in school, either."

"She doesn't mention any," Julia added.

Dora frowned. "Too bad she's alone. I've met several lonely people this holiday season. Anyone with a caring family is truly blessed."

Lana invited them into her modest eclectic style home. Dora caught sight of a few quilts, one draped across a chair and the other on her couch. Albums filled with pictures of wedding cakes she had made were displayed on the coffee table for convenient perusal. Alexia flipped through an album while her mother and Dora turned the pages of another. Alexia complimented Lana several times on her artistry. "I don't know how you turn a cake into a masterpiece. I'm lucky to even get one frosted."

Lana smiled, illuminating her somber face. "I enjoy creating," was all she said.

"I wasn't sure what I wanted before I came, but I see now I would like a traditional wedding cake with the tiers decorated with flowers."

"You will be married before Christmas?" Lana asked.

"I will."

"Are you thinking of poinsettias?"

Alexia nodded.

"Would you be interested in edible poinsettias cascading down the side of the cake?" Lana turned to a picture of a sample wedding cake.

"You can create the poinsettias out of icing?"

"I can."

"Yes, I like your suggestion. They would go with the entire theme of my wedding." Alexia caught her breath. "I can't wait to see the completed cake."

Lana pushed her overgrown brown bangs to the side and opened a note pad. "How many layers and what kind of flavor would you like them to be."

Alexia shrugged. "I don't know for sure about the number of layers, but I would like the traditional white wedding cake as moist as possible with a creamy white frosting."

"We'll get back to you on the layers," Julia told her. "We are still receiving Rsvp's."

"I take pride in making my customers happy. I'll make you a white layer cake for you to sample to see if it's to your satisfaction."

Alexia gasped. "Oh, I didn't mean to sound critical or difficult."

"I do this for all my customers. There's nothing worse than an unpalatable wedding cake."

The ladies laughed. They had eaten enough wedding cakes to know what she meant.

Lana held her long hair out of her face while she leaned over the albums. "Choose a layer shape and decide if you would like pillars between the layers."

After flipping through several photos, Alexia selected round layers with no pillars and indicated she liked the scroll work with the flowers. "What I have chosen won't be too difficult, will it?"

"No, you are doing just fine."

"Good, I don't want to get carried away on my choices."

"Anything special for the cake topper?"

Alexia laughed. "A few more flowers. No bride or groom or wedding bells. I don't want to retreat that far back in time."

Lana's expression didn't change. "Wonderful. I believe I have all I need to know for now. Anything else I can help you with?"

"I believe we are good for now," Alexia said. "Call me if there are any problems."

On their way back to the house, Alexia and Julia chatted about the cake selection. Dora retreated in thought thinking to herself there was something about Lana that seemed familiar.

Dora awakened the next morning with Ellen on her mind. She knew little about this mysterious lady, but Dora was drawn to her. Why would an aging woman live in such an isolated place? There were no neighbors that she had seen although Ellen said someone brought her supplies. Dora wanted to find out more about her. Perhaps even convince her to move to town. She had already delivered her a basket, but she decided to bake a batch of Christmas cookies to take to her, thinking they could sit and have a cup of tea with them. Perhaps this time they could visit about spiritual things. Ellen had been quick to point out that Jesus is found in the hearts of believers.

Dora reached in her refrigerator for pre-made sugar cookie dough to speed up the process. She rolled it out and used her antique cookie cutters to cut holiday shapes. She cut out several angels, thinking Ellen would appreciate them the most. After baking them, she let them cool, frosted them, and dusted them with colored sprinkles. Satisfied with their appearance, she then searched through her pantry for a cookie tin in which to arrange the decorated sugar cookies she had made. Finding one, she arranged the cookies in layers. Milton was out looking for old doors for the Christmas tree guild project. He said he would be gone all day, allowing Dora to take her time on the drive out to Ellen's.

The sun shone brightly, and the roads were dry and clear. Dora caught herself humming Christmas carols and thinking of holiday fudge. As she pulled into Ellen's driveway, she noticed the kitchen curtains had been pulled shut. Her heart sank, fearing Ellen was not home. She would have called beforehand, but Ellen had no phone.

But where would Ellen go? She asked herself. Or could she even drive? She didn't know. Ellen had never mentioned going anywhere. Leaving the cookie tin on the seat, Dora left the car and knocked on the door. She rapped several times, but there was no answer. She even tried the door knob but the house was locked. She walked around the house and peered in the living room window, seeing nothing unusual. The garage drew her attention. The swinging double doors were slightly ajar. She peeked in to see it vacant. Satisfied Ellen was not home, she wrote a brief note and placed it in the cookie tin and placed it near the front door. Deflated, she drove back to Hedge City, wondering if Ellen disappeared like she had before.

―――

When Dora finished the bridesmaids' dresses, and the girls had come by for fittings, she was free to pursue the Nativity quilt. She had called all the guild ladies together to begin the construction. She wasn't sure how to approach the project but felt confident that together they would reach a decision. The patterns she had collected and the new ones she created along with the fabric ones she had cut out were in her sewing bag.

She left sandwiches and a pot of chili for Milton's lunch. He had found several old doors at a salvage yard to cut in triangle Christmas tree shapes which would keep him busy for the day.

Most of the women who had volunteered had finished their Christmas guild quilts; although a few quilters admitted that their quilts weren't full size. Dora thanked them profusely for assisting her in this project.

She showed them the templates and explained that she wasn't able to find Jesus or the manager and she had to make a pattern. One woman suggested they leave Jesus for the last just in case the original pattern turned up. Dora had no hope that would happen but didn't comment. Thinking of what Ellen had said to her earlier, she smiled and prayed each lady would discover Jesus and the Nativity in a special way this Christmas season.

The major decision was how to make the scenes in panels and then join them together in one unit. Lily, who often drew out her quilt patterns, sketched several versions for the quilt. Since few of the quilters could meet together for long sessions of appliqué and quilting, the group decided it would be best to create the quilt in sections either individually or with two ladies or more working together. Lily drew out seven panels. The top three panels would be of the angels and the star. The middle three panels would be of Mary with the angel, the Nativity in the stable, and the third of Joseph and the angel, and the bottom panel would be of the Wise Men traveling to Bethlehem.

"But how are we going to replicate the original quilt if we don't have it," Cindy, one of the quilters, asked.

"We'll make our own quilt, use the patterns we have, and not worry about the original," Dora said. "I don't think I will be able to find the final pieces. But that's okay."

Dora asked for volunteers for the different sections. Ordinarily, two women paired up for each section, except for the last panel when three women volunteered. The ladies saved the Nativity stable scene for Dora and Josie, not realizing that Josie wouldn't be coming back from Iowa for several more weeks.

Dora handed out the templates she had collected to the appropriate group of women while giving a brief explanation where she had found them. Dora urged that each group of ladies design their own section, using the vintage patterns she had found. She told them it was her panel that contained the missing patterns.

Lily determined the size of each panel to be made. The ladies decided that each scene would be divided by narrow sashing. Dora was chosen to shop for the background material since the quilt was her idea. Lily volunteered to cut the sections from the fabric Dora chose and to distribute them to each group.

After the meeting concluded, Dora visited the town's fabric shop for the background material. She purchased beige and a dark blue fabric to resemble the night sky. She saw no need to purchase any more material since there were plenty of scraps from previous quilts for the figures and stable.

By the time she reached home, self-doubt descended like a dark cloud. For starters, Josie wouldn't be there to help, and she wasn't sure she would do the Nativity scene justice. When would she have the time? Who could help her? She couldn't do it alone. Milton had experience with quilts but probably not appliqué, and then she remembered Lana Duncan, the cake decorator, who obviously had talent even with quilts. Should she ask her to help?

―――

The next day, Dora sat down at her sewing table with the vintage templates in her hand. Baby Jesus, the manger, the stable, and the animals were absent, but she had already researched how she would replace them. Being a retired English teacher, she grasped the symbolism. Baby Jesus absent for Christmas? Replacing him?

She had a conversation with Milton the previous night, expressing her need for a quilting partner and an unclear idea how to proceed with her portion of the quilt. She had bluntly asked if Milton could assist her, but he turned her down. "I don't have the experience with appliqué," he said, although he gave her a few pointers on her Nativity scene, suggesting she begin with the stable outline.

Disappointed but not deterred, Dora found an idea for a stable online the next morning. Milton kissed her as she was huddled over the sewing machine and left her for the garage to work on his re-purposed vintage doors.

She drew out the stable outline and cut it from brown material and spent the entire morning appliquéing it on her fabric. Now all she had to do was add Joseph, Mary, Jesus, the manager and a few animals. The angels were already taken care of. The Wise Men, which would appear in the bottom panel, wouldn't be included in her scene, since they would arrive at a different place and time when baby Jesus was older.

Dora finished the final stitch when Milton came in for lunch. "How's it going?" he asked his wife as she was dishing up stew from the crock pot.

"The stable is done. How's your project?"

"You must come out and see."

She filled the bowls with the steamy aroma of basil, tender meat, carrots, and potatoes. "I will. Right after lunch."

"I think you'll be pleased with my first tree."

"I'm sure I will."

"How many trees should I make? I have one door left."

"Two should be adequate."

Before they finished with lunch, Dora answered the phone. It was Alexia. "Dora I need help at the daycare again. I must have a day off to go shopping for wedding things."

"Can't you find someone else? I don't have Josie here to help out."

"I'll have a friend who's licensed. Follow her lead. Do what you did when I was there."

"If I remember it was long hours." She hesitated. "We began work on the Nativity quilt," Dora added.

"One more day. I promise I won't ask you again."

Dora rolled her eyes and mouthed the conversation to Milton. He shrugged.

"Well, okay, when do you want me?"

"The day after tomorrow, please and thank you."

Alexia ended the conversation before Dora could reconsider. She turned to Milton with a look of defeat. "I have to find a quilter to help me with this Nativity quilt. I will never get it done at this rate."

Milton blotted his lips with the napkin. "Call Josie and tell her to come back pronto."

Dora shook her head. "No, can't do that, but I was thinking of asking Lana Duncan, the woman who will bake Alexia's cake if she could help."

"She makes quilts, too?"

"She does. In fact, I might call her this afternoon."

He took Dora's hand. "Not until you see my Christmas tree."

"Let's have a look."

"I don't have the tree stand made yet. I sanded on the cut sides just before lunch." He paused as if to give her time for a good look.

"I like it. It's simple, and it's apple green. It reminds me of my mother's kitchen. She painted everything that color."

Milton chuckled. "Including the doors. It wasn't simple to cut." He pointed out the rough edges. "They made these doors of solid wood. Hard wood at that."

"I wonder if we should add a little decoration to it. Nothing ostentatious. A little garland or a star."

"I'll let you take care of decorating. I have another door to cut."

She directed her attention to the other door. "White," she said. "It will work nicely, too. Good work, Milton." She patted him on the back.

He smiled at her compliment.

"After I wash dishes, I'm calling Lana to see if I can come over."

"I'll be here," he said, picking up the saw.

Dora called Lana as soon as she returned to the house and confirmed a time to come over. She placed the dishes in the dishwasher and cleaned the counter and then left the house.

"Did you have changes for the wedding cake?" Lana asked when she answered the door.

"No, I wanted to speak to you about quilts."

Lana looked bewildered and invited her to have a seat in the living room. "What did you have in mind?"

"I'm afraid I've overextended my commitments," Dora frowned. "Josie and I have already made a poinsettia quilt for the quilt show. She left for Iowa and won't be back for another two weeks. In the meantime, I've discovered vintage templates for a Nativity quilt." She shrugged. "For some reason, I decided to make this quilt for the church. Since Josie is gone, I need a partner quilter to finish my assigned portion of the quilt."

"It sounds like you're busy."

"Alexia needs help at her daycare, so that limits my time."

Lana tugged at her blouse. "And you want me to help you out?"

"Yes, I realize you're busy, too, but working together we could get the portion done in a week. We have divided the quilt into sections and have assigned two or three women to a section."

"What would I be doing?"

"The stable scene. I have the stable outline finished." Dora hesitated. "You'd help with appliqué." She held her breath.

"I can appliqué. What method will you use?"

"Fusible webbing."

"I can do that."

"Good. The layout will be up to us. I haven't found the original quilt or even a photo. In fact, we don't have all the templates."

"Sounds like an ambitious project."

"It is, but eleven women have volunteered to help."

"Where would we work?"

"At my house for most of the sewing until we are ready to join the sections together."

"I'd be willing to assist you. I only have Alexia's wedding cake and two Christmas cakes to make. I should be able to squeeze in a quilt section."

"Wonderful. Thanks so much."

"When do we start?"

"How about the day after tomorrow? I'm helping at the daycare tomorrow."

"Call me, and I'll come over."

Dora thanked her and let herself out, thinking Lana didn't even smile once. At first she had felt presumptuous asking a near stranger to share a quilting project, but now she thought perhaps she was meant to spend time with Lana.

———

The licensed daycare worker Alexia had chosen to assist Dora at the daycare appeared a little older than Dora. She arrived with a large box of Kleenex and a can of disinfectant spray. As soon as she entered the room, she sprayed a steady stream of droplets until the children coughed and covered their faces. Realizing she may have overdone it, Delores explained that she was susceptible to cold germs and didn't want to be sick for Christmas. Dora sympathized with her and passed her the hand sanitizer.

Being familiar with the day's schedule, Dora started the routine. Delores poured herself a cup of coffee from her thermos and sat down at the table while Dora scrambled to gather the children together for story time. "Would you like to read the story?" Dora asked Delores, breathlessly.

"Oh I can't," she said. "I have cataracts, and I'm unable to see the words."

Dora accepted her excuse and attempted to settle in a child's chair but gave up and pulled a folding chair near the story circle. She wished she was familiar with the story. Reading upside down proved a challenge, but she made it through with a little ad-libbing. She looked over her shoulder to see if Delores noticed, but she had pulled a doughnut out of her purse and was nibbling. Dora rolled her eyes, realizing Delores would be no help unless breakfast rejuvenated her.

Alexia ran her daycare more like a preschool, Dora thought. Alexia didn't believe in wasting time when there was an opportunity to teach. Dora agreed and was aware of teachable moments.

By reading the list of activities, Dora learned developing large motor skills was important to Alexia. Usually, the children played in the fenced back yard, but it was too cold to venture out, so Alexia had suggested a few indoor games. Duck, duck, goose was one on the list. Dora wasn't sure how to play it, so she asked Delores for help. Delores explained the process but when Dora asked Delores to demonstrate, she waved her hand. "I can't run anymore."

Running wasn't Dora's strong suit anymore either, but she did the best she could to make the children comfortable with the game. After several rounds were played, Dora stopped to catch her breath. "What next?" she asked herself as she checked Alexia's list.

Snack time. She dashed in the kitchen to fetch the snacks Alexia had prepared for the children. While they ate, she attempted a breather which didn't last long. One child spilled his milk; another dropped her fruit cup on the floor. By the time she rectified the situations, snack time was over.

Thankfully, free play time at the centers was next. She prayed the children could entertain themselves for fifteen minutes while she checked the schedule for the next event. Music came next. Dora implored Delores to help her. She was sure Delores would claim a sore throat, but Dora was prepared to beg. Delores formed the words, "I'm sorry—" Dora cut her off with "I beg you to take charge of the music, so I can prepare for the next task." Delores shrugged and gathered the children together and then sat at the piano and played the music while the children sang like angels. Dora glowered and began to think unkind thoughts while trying her hardest to adopt the Christian attitude. "Forgive me, Father," she whispered.

While music was in progress, she looked at the schedule. Lunch! Oh, dear how was she going to prepare lunch and supervise the children at the same time? Delores will have to step up. Dora explained the situation to Delores, giving her the option of preparing lunch or supervising. Delores frowned. "I know nothing about this kitchen. I'll supervise."

"Fine," Dora said under her breath and hurried to the kitchen to prepare sandwiches and veggies. The noise decimals rose by the minute in the outer room. She peeked around the doorway to see the children out of control, throwing toys and chasing each other while screaming. Should she say something to Delores who was supposed to be a licensed daycare worker? She counted to ten and clamped her jaw.

It took awhile to settle the children before eating lunch. By now Dora was exhausted. She was too tired to eat; and a headache threatened; however, Delores had no trouble consuming several sandwiches and producing several cookies from her purse that weren't on the menu. Doris clenched her mouth and tried not to judge her. Perhaps she was tired, too and really didn't want to be here, either.

Nap time followed lunch. At last, a respite, Dora thought. Delores reclined on the couch when the children dutifully spread out their rugs and lay down while soft music played in the background. Dora sat in the rocking chair and closed her eyes only to be awakened by a three-year-old needing a soft lap. Surprised that a child would choose her as a surrogate mother, she let the little girl snuggle in and fall asleep. The bliss of rest lasted for forty-five minutes when the tikes stirred. She herself had dozed off for a few minutes. What would Alexia say? Dora quickly got up with the child still in her arms. The schedule? What was next? Hadn't they done everything already?

Dora pulled the sheet of activities from her pocket. Alexia had jotted down another story time. Since the children were still a little sleepy, she deduced reading a book would be a snap. She looked to Delores to take this task over but saw that Delores had left for the kitchen.

Sighing deeply, Dora opened the book and read. Several of the children yawned and rubbed their eyes. Dora's eyes became heavy and she yawned, too, while sneaking a peek at the clock. The daycare closed at five. Only three and a half hours left.

Free play followed the story. The children became active then and ran to their favorite play center. Dora brewed coffee in the kitchen while Delores sat in a chair and supervised. According to the schedule, crafts came next. Alexia presented Dora with an option, either finger painting or a paper plate activity. Painting with the fingers nauseated Dora. She chose the paper plate craft and didn't give it another thought.

Dora poured two cups of coffee and brought one to Delores who was nodding off in the chair. Curious as to Delores's daycare past, she nestled in the chair beside her and asked her questions. She began as nonchalantly as she could. "How many years have you been a daycare provider?"

"Not too many. After my husband died, I had to provide for myself. My daughter suggested daycare. I had taken care of my four grandchildren when they were little." Delores plucked another cookie from her purse. "She felt I was qualified. Becoming licensed insured me a better chance for work, so I went through the course work."

"Now, you fill in?"

"Rarely. Alexia begged me, so I agreed to help her out for a day."

Two girls fought over a pair of dress-up shoes. Delores made no attempt to move. Dora set her cup down and arbitrated the dispute. And since she was already moving about, she laid out the materials for the Christmas paper plate craft and then approached Delores. "I've little experience doing a craft with small children. I need your expert help, please."

"It's not that hard," Delores said from her sitting position. "Don't you have grandkids?"

94

"Well, it is for me," Dora retorted rather harshly, not answering her question.

Delores frowned and pushed herself out of the chair.

As Dora suspected most of the children showed difficulty cutting and pasting. At least, she thought, Delores could help with that. At least an hour passed before the children completed their Santa Claus renditions. "Ho, Ho, Ho," Dora said to the little ones as she decorated the classroom windows with their projects.

By then the children were ready for a snack. Dora handed out small packets of fruit snacks. A few more songs were sung before the parents arrived between four and five to pick up their kids. In the meantime, Dora tidied up the rooms for the next day. She and Delores left as soon as the last child departed.

Dora couldn't wait to get home and flop in her recliner. Milton had called her and said he had purchased a pizza for supper. Good, she thought on her way home, no need to cook. Dora met Milton just as he was pulling into the driveway with their supper. "Thanks for planning ahead," she told her husband. "All I can think of is getting off my feet." He smiled and wrapped his arm around her waist and walked her into the house with instructions to rest. She changed into her robe and settled into her chair just in time for the pizza that Milton had brought into the living room.

"I finished the second tree," he said after he took his first bite. "But you can wait to see it tomorrow."

"Thanks. I'm sure it's grand." She reached for another pizza slice. "Which one do you like the best?"

"Hard to tell until you put on your finishing touches."

"Whatever that will be." Dora quickly sat up straight. "Someone's at the door."

Milton set down his half-eaten pizza and answered the knock. Dora heard Alexia's voice. "I'm in here," she yelled out.

"I came by to see how your day went. I see you're beat."

Dora eyed her sternly. "Where did you come up with Delores?"

"Why do you ask?"

"She lacked ambition and a sense of duty."

Alexia cowered. "Are you mad at me?"

"I survived, but please don't pair us together again."

"I'm sorry. My neighbor mentioned her, and I was desperate."

"I figured as much."

"Not to worry. I shouldn't be asking you again." Alexia pecked her on the cheek. "I appreciate your help immensely."

"And what did you do today?"

"John was fitted for his tux. I ordered our flowers and the greenery to decorate the church. I bought the stuff for the invitations." Alexia tapped her chin. "Ah, yes, I looked for table decorations."

"You've found a place for the reception?"

"Not yet."

"Hope that won't be a problem."

"Me, too. I'd better run. Just wanted to see how you were. Thanks again."

Milton pointed to the coffee table. "Want a slice of pizza?"

"Thanks." Alexia grabbed a slice and let herself out.

"Nice niece you got there," Milton said.

"She is. I wouldn't have substituted with Delores at daycare for just anybody."

Dora slept in late the next morning. Milton was already in the garage and had left a plate of pancakes and a pot of coffee for her. She downed two cups of coffee before she ventured to the garage to see Milton's tree. He was working on the tree stands when she entered.

"Hi, sleepy head," he teased her.

"Thanks for letting me sleep. Now where's that tree you made?"

He pointed to the floor. "I'll set it up, so you can see." He picked up scraps from the floor. "I'm making a stand for it."

She studied his creation. "The white gives the illusion that the tree has been flocked. Adding small red twinkling lights and a star would work."

"When should we take the two trees over to the quilt show venue?"

"I would think anytime. We may have to buy something to decorate them with. I don't know what's left in my decorating box."

"Let's check first before we go shopping."

"Yes, a good idea." She shuffled her feet. "I've been thinking about driving over to Rock Falls and see if Ellen Good is home."

"You want to drive thirty miles round trip just to check on her?"

"I do. I'm concerned why she left when she said she didn't get out much."

He scrunched his face. "I'll go with you as soon as I screw together a tree stand. Why don't you search through your Christmas decorations and see if you have something to dress up these wooden trees."

"Okay." She blew him a kiss. "Thanks Milton."

While she sorted through the unused decorations, she heard his drill screeching from the garage. She shook her head at the noise and then pulled out useable garland and one shabby star from the box. She picked up the silver garland and joined Milton in the garage.

"Found something?"

"Garland and a star, nothing else."

She draped the garland on the green wood and wrinkled her nose. "That won't do. We must go shopping."

"When we get back from Rock Falls, we'll stop at the store." He stood back and admired his trees standing upright on the home made tree stands. "I'm ready," he said.

When they pulled into Ellen Good's drive-way, Dora's face fell. "She's not home."

"I believe you're right. Let's get out and have a look."

They walked up to the front door. Dora let out a cry. "The cookie tin I brought her is still here." She bent down, picked it up, and opened it. Seeing the cookies still looked edible, she bit into one and handed Milton another. "Where could she be?"

Milton shrugged. "Are there any neighbors around here that might know her whereabouts?"

"I don't know."

"I suggest we drive around and see if we can find any."

"What should I do with the cookies?"

"Bring them along. I don't see any sense wasting good food."

Milton explored the dirt side roads which wound around deserted and dilapidated buildings. "Looks like a ghost town. Curious that Ellen Good would want to live in such a place. She doesn't even have a dog to keep her company."

"Makes little sense to me, either."

"Hold on a minute." Milton pointed. "See that cabin over there with the woodpile beside it?"

"I do. I see smoke."

Milton drove up to the log building. "Shall we see if someone lives here?"

"If you come with me."

"Of course."

Milton led the way to the log cabin. He knocked on the door and waited. Soon a grizzled old man with shabby gray hair and beard answered. He stared at them and didn't say a word.

Milton cleared his throat and introduced them before he spoke. "We're looking for Ellen Good. She's not home, and we were wondering if you knew where she is."

"Why should I know?"

Milton straightened his shoulders. Today, he was not a man to be intimidated. "You seem to be her only neighbor."

"Just because we both live in the same town doesn't mean we're neighbors."

"You admit you know her?"

"Sure, I know who she is, and I'm not about to tell you anything about her." He shut the door in their faces. Milton and Dora stood shocked for a moment and retreated to the car.

"Well of all the nerve," Dora stormed as she fastened her seat belt.

"Did Ellen every mention him?"

"Ellen told me that someone got her supplies, and I bet someone also chops her wood."

"Two recluses that live in the same ghost town," Milton mused.

"I'd say there's an interesting story here."

Since it was late when Milton and Dora arrived back at Hedge City, they postponed their trip to the store until the next morning. Over breakfast, they discussed the strange vibes they felt after talking to the man who lived in the cabin.

"He knows where she is," Dora said vehemently.

"I agree but he's not about to tell us. I sense he's protecting her for some reason."

"How are we going to find out?"

"It's none of our business, Dora."

"Wonder if he's done something to her?"

"You're letting your imagination run wild."

"How do you know?"

"Call it detective's instinct."

She glared at him and said nothing more.

Milton reached for her hand. "If it makes you feel any better, we'll drive out there next week."

"Thank you."

"Do you still want to shop?"

"I feel a little faint."

"Understandable. The old gent was a little scary." His eyes held concern. "Shake it off and breathe deeply."

"Okay. I'll try." She shuddered. "Then we can deliver your trees to the quilt guild. I understand they will work today at the community hall."

"I'll load the trees. You can decorate them at the hall?"

"I will."

Buying red lights, candy stripe garland, and two new stars at the local hardware store restored Dora's enthusiasm. She calmed, especially when she viewed how the Community Center transformed into a green, red, and white quilt paradise.

100

Some quilters had already brought in their completed quilts and displayed them clipped to a web of wires. Many were appliqué but patchwork reigned. Dora visualized the poinsettia quilt adding another dimension to the Christmas theme. She studied the few displayed antique quilts that had been stored in cedar chests for years and had rarely seen daylight. Moving in closer, she caught the faint scent of cedar.

Milton set up the wooden door trees among the other unique Christmas trees, some made from horseshoes, barbed wire, and tumble weeds. Imagination escaped none of them. Dora studied Milton's trees and thought less ornamentation would showcase his trees the best. With Milton's help, Dora placed a white star and the red and white candy striped garland on the light green tree. Dora smiled as she handed Milton a red star and red twinkling lights for the white tree. When it was finished Milton let out a low whistle. "Perfect."

Dora glanced at her watch. "We've time for a quick lunch, and then Lana is coming over to begin the quilt. What do you have planned for this afternoon?"

"Don't know. Shall I do more baking?"

"How are you at making fudge?"

"I've done it before, peanut brittle, too?"

"Would you like to use my recipes or do you have your own?"

Milton grimaced. "I'll use yours. I have no idea what recipe I even used."

Shorty after lunch, Lana arrived. The ladies slipped off to the living room and left Milton to the kitchen. Dora explained that she had already cut out a few of the figures, although they wouldn't be able to use all of them. "I got ahead of myself," she admitted.

Dora showed her the stable she had already appliquéd on the fabric, explaining Lily had pre-cut the background for all of them to use for their portions of the quilt. "Now all we have to do is fill in the stable with Mary, Joseph, and baby Jesus. The shepherds and sheep will stand to the side."

"And where do you want me to begin?" Lana asked.

"With Mary. Are you familiar with fusible webbing?"

"I am."

Dora laid out the patterns on the colors she had chosen. "Good. You can either draw the patterns on the paper side of the webbing and do the cutting, or you can do the stitching once it's adhered to the fabric?"

"I'd rather you do the stitching," Lana said.

"I don't mind." Dora pushed the Mary pattern over to Lana. "We'll start here first. Once that is sewed on we will have eight more patterns left."

Once Lana traced the pattern on the paper side of the webbing, she cut around it, leaving a two inch margin. Then she placed the pattern on the blue fabric and ironed it until the sticky side adhered. She cut it out and handed it to Dora who positioned it on the background fabric after insuring it was centered. Dora had changed her thread to blue and zigzagged the edges of Mary.

When they became comfortable with the process, they visited.

"I appreciate your help." Dora smiled briefly. "Have you considered joining our guild?"

Lana traced Joseph on the webbing. "No... I'm busy with my cake decorating business. Quilting comes second."

"Where did you learn the art of cake decorating? I admire anyone who can make a wedding cake."

"My mother taught me the rudiments. I liked it so well I signed up for cake decorating courses."

"I'm happy someone has the talent. I can't seem to keep a steady hand when I try to decorate which is seldom."

"We have our own talents," Lana said without emotion as she cut around Joseph robed in light tan.

Even though Lana was reticent, Dora wanted to learn more about her. She kept asking questions. "I don't remember you from school. You didn't always live here did you?"

"I grew up in Omaha. When I married, we moved to Hedge City."

"I don't remember having any of your children in school."

"We didn't have children."

Dora felt like she had asked enough, but she wanted to know about her husband and where he had worked. She didn't remember him at all. Thinking she had probed enough, she fell silent.

Lana left at four o'clock, since Dora and Milton had their last Cantata practice that evening. Both enjoyed singing the Christmas music and agreed participating added joy to the Christmas season. After Dora's conversation with Ellen, Dora had become more immersed in the spiritual significance of Christmas. The cantata music they had practiced for weeks was beautiful and had brought her a sense of peace, but did she really savor the words along with the musical notes? Each line, often a verse of Scripture, spoke to her in a way it had never before.

After practice, Dora and Milton tried on choir robes for the final performance. "I haven't worn one of these since college," Dora remarked. "I find taking part in the cantata an inspirational experience," she said to Milton. "Thanks for sharing the joy with me."

His eyes twinkled. "My pleasure."

With the blue and white robes in hand, Dora and Milton left for home, singing Handel's Hallelujah chorus.

"God be praised," Dora rejoiced.

———

When Dora and Lana met for their next quilting session, she invited her to the cantata. From visiting, Dora surmised Lana led a self-imposed, isolated life.

"Thank you, but I'm busy that evening," Lana told her.

"You must come. The music is absolutely inspiring and beautiful."

Lana smoothed the pattern of an angel on the webbing. "I... don't really appreciate religious music."

Lana's comment stunned her. She had just assumed Lana was associated with one of the three churches in town. After all she was making a Nativity quilt. Suddenly Dora realized what she had asked of her. "How do you feel about making this Nativity quilt?"

"Okay. It's a nice story."

"The most important story ever told," Dora said slightly offended. Here was her opportunity to witness but all of a sudden she was at a loss for words. *What can I say to her that would make a difference?* "You're not a believer?" She asked too abruptly.

"No, I'm in charge of my life, the successes and the failures. They're my doing?"

104

Dora hesitated. "You don't believe God is our creator, and that he sent his son into the world on Christmas?"

Lana shook her head.

"You've never been to church or Sunday school?"

"I went with my parents every Sunday, but when I found out I was adopted the Sunday school teachings didn't mean that much anymore."

Adopted? Dora didn't expect this for a reason for her lack of faith. She wasn't sure she should probe anymore.

Lana cut the angel from shimmery white fabric and passed it to Dora to be stitched. Dora's hands shook as she reached for it.

"Would you rather have someone else work on the quilt with you? Someone who believes?" Lana asked.

"No, the idea hasn't crossed my mind. I assume you are familiar with the Nativity?"

"Sure, I know it as well as anyone."

"You must know that it's true."

"Why did God take my real mother away from me? Explain that." Lana sat rigid. "Why am I alone? Why did I do things that I regret?"

"Your adoptive parents weren't good to you?"

"They were okay, but I don't think they really loved me. Although, I don't know what love is for sure."

Dora trembled. "I'm not great explaining why bad things happen in the world. But I know God has a purpose for everything, and he forgives us if we are truly repentant." Frantically she searched her memory for Scripture, praying silently as she racked her brain. "Romans 8:28 reads, 'We know that all things work together for the good of those who love God, who are called according to his purpose.'"

"It's all too confusing. I just don't know."

Dora smiled. "Come to the cantata. You'll experience a feeling of peace and joy."

"I'll think about it."

"Milton and I can pick you up if you rather not go alone."

"Like I said, I'll think about it."

Dora nodded, realizing that was all she could do for now. God would have to open her heart. "Want to complete one more pattern before we call it a day?"

"Fine with me. I'd like to see this done before I make Alexia's wedding cake."

Dora had sewed Mary and Joseph in the stable. Baby Jesus and the manger should be next, but she hesitated and chose the shepherd templates and gave them to Lana. "Let's do one of these before we end for the day."

"Shouldn't Jesus come next?" Lana asked.

"I'm hoping to find the original. If I don't, then I'll use the template from another quilt."

"Jesus is lost?"

"Jesus is in the heart of believers. Only the template is lost." Dora's heart thumped against her chest surprised those words came out of her mouth.

Lana said nothing but looked at her puzzled.

After Lana left, Dora straightened up the living room. Both agreed to meet again in a couple of days to work on the quilt.

Milton came home from stringing wires for the quilts at the quilt show venue. "Looks to be a success. We have to add more spaces."

"Wonderful. Our poinsettia quilt is done. I must pick it up and add it to the show."

Milton helped with supper by opening the cans of soup while she toasted the sandwiches.

Over a meal of tomato soup and toasted cheese sandwiches Dora told Milton about her day. "Have you ever thought people often masquerade as someone different from who they truly are?"

"In my profession it happens all the time."

"O f course, I should have thought of that."

Milton wiped the soup from his lips. "Why do you ask?"

"If you had to describe Lana Duncan to someone, what would you say?"

"She seems like a nice lady dedicated to her skills although I surmise she likes to spend time alone."

"I would've said the same thing." Dora ladled more soup into their bowls while Milton waited for Dora to continue. "This afternoon Lana opened up a little more than she has before. We got on the subject of religion because of the Nativity quilt, and she admitted she is not a believer."

"Not everyone is."

"I assumed she was since she agreed to help me with the quilt. She told me she considers the Nativity a nice story. Emphasis on story." Dora dropped the spoon on her plate. "And there's more."

Milton raised his head. "Oh?"

"She's adopted and attributes her lack of faith on being given up for adoption. Can you imagine after all these years?"

"She didn't love her adoptive parents? Were they abusive?"

"That's just it. Lana claims she never felt loved, but she was never abused."

"You've never taken such interest in someone else before. What gives?"

107

Dora shrugged. "I don't know. I feel sorry for all the lonely people in this town."

"They've probably been here all along."

"You're right, and I've ignored them."

Milton reached for her hand. "Now don't be hard on yourself. We all become preoccupied with our own lives."

"Pastor reminded us that Christmas is a season for loving and giving. I'm not sure I've done that well over the years."

"Did you know Lana's adoptive parents?"

"No, they lived in Omaha. Lana moved here with her husband although she didn't say much about him. They had no children."

"Would you like me to research him?" Milton pushed the empty bowl aside. "What's his first name?"

"I don't know."

"Then let's visit the cemetery tomorrow."

"And pick up the poinsettia quilt. I hope it turned out okay."

Light snow was falling when Dora and Milton awoke the next morning. "Not a good day to go headstone hunting," Dora mumbled from beneath the covers.

"It's just a little snow, Dora. Where's your sense of adventure?"

"By the fireplace."

"I'll make breakfast while you get ready. Dress Warm," he called after her.

Sometimes, she disliked it when Milton was too cheerful. Their attitudes for early morning hours were different, she thought to herself when she forced herself out of bed and into the shower. She heard Milton humming in the kitchen and smelled the aroma of morning coffee.

By the time she dried off and wrapped her fluffy robe around her, Milton had placed a breakfast of waffles, fruit, and coffee on the table. "Thanks for breakfast, Milton." She sat at the table and reached for her coffee.

"You're most welcome," he said while passing the waffles to her.

"Anthony called while you were in the shower. They plan on coming within a week."

"Wonderful. I miss Josie so much. She could have helped me with the quilt, but then I wouldn't have had the chance to get to know Lana." She frowned. "Not that I really know her."

"Leave it to me. We'll get answers."

After breakfast, Dora shooed Milton off for a shower while she loaded the dishwasher and dressed for their outing. In forty-five minutes, they were on their way to the cemetery. Cemeteries were no strangers to the couple. While investigating mysteries, they had visited several for important genealogical information. There was only one in Hedge City.

The cemetery was small compared to many they had visited and held a veil of light snow. Dora and Milton split company, each taking a half section of the graveyard. "I assume we're looking for the surname Duncan, unless... unless Lana changed her name back to Duncan after her husband died." Dora said.

Milton chuckled. "Now you're thinking like a detective."

In a half-hour Dora spotted a single, small headstone with the name of Duncan. She waved Milton over to her side. "This could be it." The first name of Roger was inscribed with the birth date and death. "He died two years ago while Josie and I were on vacation."

"Did you know Roger at all?"

"No, I didn't. Strange that I wouldn't have. He probably didn't live here long."

Milton stroked his chin. "And I find it unusual that he would be buried here in Hedge City. I didn't think I would find him here."

"Really?"

"He didn't seem to be well known in this area. Wouldn't a person be interred where the relatives and friends lived?"

"True. At least now you have a name to start with."

"I'll enter it and see what we find."

"Don't forget to stop for the poinsettia quilt."

Milton nodded and drove several blocks from the cemetery.

Dora fell in love with the quilt when she saw it. The quilting gave the poinsettias a depth of beauty Alexia would surely appreciate, too. Since she was eager to see what it would look like with the other quilts, she talked Milton in stopping by the quilt venue and putting it up on the wire before they returned home. Milton had already selected a special place for it, so it could be seen immediately when the visitors arrived.

Once the quilt was displayed, Dora stood back and marveled.

"It's a masterpiece, Dora," Milton said. "You and Josie did a wonderful job."

"No, it's you who is the masterpiece," she said. "Now, let's go, so you can get on your computer.

Back at the house, Dora brewed a pot of coffee while Milton settled into his computer. She had just loaded a plate with cookies when Milton called, "Come here, Dora, I found something."

Stars glittered brilliantly in the night sky as Dora and Milton carried their choir robes to the car. Dora had just popped a throat lozenge in her mouth to prepare for the concert. "Hope you're not getting a cold," Milton commented in concern.

"Stage fright. I think." She wondered who would attend the cantata. She had invited everyone she knew, including her friends at the rest home and Lana. Usually, the rest home transported the able residents to such events.

Upon arrival, Dora and Milton went backstage and donned their choir robes over their street clothes. Soon every choir member looked similar but festive. Their conductor gave them last-minute instructions with a thumb up, and then they filed out and stepped onto the risers. Dora wobbled as she ascended to the second riser and grabbed a hold of the nearest alto.

The musical arrangement began with Handel's most familiar Messiah pieces. She looked over the audience and felt faint when she saw Lana Duncan. She praised God for preparing Lana's heart for this moment. Dora knew she wasn't responsible for her attendance or any change that might take place. It was God's doing, and she rejoiced.

She saw Alexia and Julia and her friends from the rest home. She was glad they were there to add brightness to their days. Suddenly, the music started, and she was jolted back to the concert. Her knees shook and her face grew warm as she sang "Comfort Ye My People."

The conductor interspersed the program with music from several sources, including another Messiah piece, "For Unto us a Child is Born." She recalled the words came from Isaiah chapter nine. The music sent chills through her as she sang and eventually the cantata culminated into the "Hallelujah Chorus." Her voice was spent by the time the cantata concluded.

Afterwards, Dora searched the crowd for Lana, but she concluded Lana apparently slipped out after it was over. Milton touched her elbow and guided her toward Alexia and Julia. "Beautiful job," Alexia gushed. "How can you sing such difficult music?" she asked of Dora and Milton.

Dora's voice grated. "This may be my last one."

"I can see why. It takes musical talent to do it justice."

"You and Milton must sing a duet at church," Julia suggested. Milton blushed.

"We have never sung together," Dora quickly added, realizing that as a couple they were still discovering each other.

The evening was early yet. Dora suggested they visit the quilt venue. "They're open for another hour, and I would like Julia and Alexia to see Josie's and my poinsettia quilt," she said to Milton.

He nodded in agreement. On the way, Dora told him she had seen Lana at the cantata. "She told me she didn't like religious music."

"She apparently changed her mind."

"I can't wait to see her again and find out what she has to say."

"Don't' get your hopes up, Dora. These things take time."

"I won't, but I consider this a breakthrough."

112

Before they entered the building, Dora challenged Julia and Alexia to find their quilt just in case there would be other poinsettia quilts displayed. Both she and Milton were astounded at the quilts added since they had been there.

"Looks like you have a hit on your hands," Julia said as she gaped at the display.

Alexia laughed in glee. "And we know where your quilt is." She pointed right to it.

"Do you like it?" Dora asked hopefully.

"Very much," Alexia said.

Dora was tempted to tell her it would be her wedding gift but remembered Josie would be cross, besides Milton looked sternly at her.

They stopped at each quilt displayed, commenting on the beauty and workmanship of each one. "Julia, do you remember the quilts our mother made?"

"Not too much. I vaguely remember one. Maybe that's why I didn't quilt like you and Josie."

"Could be," Dora mused as she led them to the unique trees where she pointed out Milton's creations. Milton acknowledged that the wood door trees were Dora's idea, but they pleased the crowd.

They concluded with the last aisle which displayed all the antique quilts. Dora had seen most all of them and wasn't prepared for the surprise which loomed ahead of her. She couldn't believe her eyes and grabbed Milton's arm for support. She pointed to the quilt with a blue background and appliquéd with the familiar biblical figures. "It's the original Nativity quilt," she gasped. "Where did it come from?" Julia and Alexia gathered around her and stared. Milton suggested that they ask the quilters in charge for the day if they had seen who had brought it in.

After Dora composed herself, she and Milton asked about the Nativity quilt. No one saw who brought the quilt. They told them they had found the quilt in the morning with a note gifting it to the quilt guild. "And no one thought to tell me?" she fired.

"We're sorry. We didn't know."

Dora apologized, realizing that these quilters had not volunteered for the Nativity quilt project, so they wouldn't know about its importance. Returning to the quilt, she studied the arrangement and patterns. "It's somewhat similar to what we have drawn out except they included the Wise Men with the stable scene." The original quilters didn't have the modern day fusible webbing, either. Instead, they turned the edges and slip stitched around the template. Quilting was done by hand.

Her eyes were drawn to Jesus and the manger, the missing pieces. The templates she would have used for Jesus and the manger were inferior to the original. "I must try to duplicate the missing templates," Dora said to her sister and niece.

"You don't have the patterns?" Julia asked puzzled.

"I've found all the templates except for Jesus, the manger, and a few animals," Dora explained. "Violet's mother, Prudence Hanson, was the last one known to have the templates."

Julia studied baby Jesus appliquéd in the quilt. "Violet doesn't have them?"

"No, she doesn't. Violet also told me that her mother wasn't one to save things. I'm afraid the pattern is gone."

"What a shame," Julia said. "There's something about this template that's...special."

"I agree," Dora said.

Dora didn't sleep well the night after seeing the original Nativity quilt. She decided she would have to find an artist to duplicate the pattern. The first thing in the morning, she would make phone calls to locate someone. She told Milton her plan over breakfast the next morning.

"Dora, you're driving yourself to distraction," Milton warned her. "Is this quilt worth the worry?"

She nodded sheepishly. "It seems silly, but I want to find out the full story of this quilt."

"And you're also obsessed with Lana and her past."

"Roger is a mystery," Dora reminded him. "Especially, when you found out they weren't even married."

"I'll do more research today and see why she claimed him as a husband."

A rap at the door interrupted their conversation. Before Dora could get up to answer, Julia barged through the door.

Alarmed, Dora abruptly left her chair almost knocking it over. "Is something wrong, Julia?"

"No, it's just that I remembered something."

Dora held her hand over her heart. "Like what?"

"You said Prudence Hanson had the missing patterns at one time."

"I did."

"I went to her estate auction when you and Josie were traveling the United States. I bought several things. One was a box of sewing items. I never took the time to look through it." Julia shrugged. "I hoped you and Josie might have a use for them."

"You did? Where are they?"

"Come over and I'll show you. I'm sorry, but I forgot I had the box."

"Have you looked inside?"

"No, I haven't."

Dora practically pushed her out the door. "Cross our fingers and let's go look."

———

Milton remained at the house while Dora accompanied Julia to her house. He was doubtful Dora would find what she was looking for. Too many years had passed. He sat down at the computer to search for Roger Duncan if that was indeed his real name. At the end of the half-hour, he decided there was no such person as Roger Duncan. The only way to find out who Roger Duncan was to ask Lana and that was unlikely she would answer.

Milton paced the floor thinking. If Roger was using an alias why would he be buried under an assumed name? Could he possibly be a fugitive? A picture of him would be useful to check against the data bases. Dora might be able to obtain a picture from Lana, but that wasn't going to happen.

Newspapers had always been helpful in his cases. He grabbed his coat and drove down to the Hedge City newspaper office. Beginning with Roger's death date, Milton worked backwards. Roger's obituary was brief and didn't reveal much information. He doubted any of it was accurate and wasn't surprised there was no picture included.

After searching through a myriad of newspapers, he concluded Lana and Roger kept to themselves and never intended to become part of the community. Just to be sure he didn't miss anything; he went back at least five years. Lana's name was mentioned only in regard to her cake decorating business. The social column never wrote about Roger and only included Lana's name in connection with a special cake. Disappointed he didn't find any clues, Milton stopped in at the local bars where he inquired if anyone knew Roger Duncan. Most of the bar tenders were young and worked only part-time except for the last bar in which he inquired. An older man known as Zeke was talkative and not intimidated by questions.

"It's been several years," Zeke said. "Roger did come in occasionally and sat by himself at the far table. He favored scotch."

"Did he meet anyone or have any friends that you knew of?"

"He was definitely a loner. Never saw him with a woman either."

Milton stroked his chin. "What did he do for a living?"

"He never said but sometimes he carried a black briefcase with him. The kind a salesperson often carries." Zeke wiped the bar. "And there was no funeral. I thought that was funny. I didn't even know he died until I read the paper."

"Did you notice his car? License plate?"

Zeke shook his head.

"Anyone else who would know something about him?"

Zeke shook his head. "Like I said that was a few years ago. He was always alone."

Milton thanked him for his help and left his number just in case he thought of something more. He had worked with enough cases to know Roger Duncan was an assumed name and had a past he had wanted to leave behind. But what was his connection with Lana who seemed to be a normal, law abiding lady.

Julia already had the box sitting on the kitchen table. "I haven't even looked through it entirely," she told Dora.

Dora's hands trembled as she opened the box. Inside were old pattern books and an assortment of quilt templates as well as a few unfinished blocks. Dora sorted through them quickly in hopes of finding baby Jesus and the manger. The missing templates could be drawn out now that they had seen the Nativity quilt, but she was hopeful of finding the original.

She opened a yellowing envelope to find a handful of old photographs and sorted through them. Most resembled Prudence's family. Young Violet was in several. "I wonder if Violet knows that these photographs exist."

"Take them to her," Julia said. "This box and everything in it belongs to you and Josie. I have no use for it."

"I will. She might like them." Dora pulled out a manila envelope marked 1950 quilt. Her heart skipped a beat. "I've found something." Hurriedly, she spilled the contents onto the table. A photograph fell out along with a notebook of sketches. The photograph drew her attention. Holding it so Julia could see, Dora identified her mother along with the other quilters. This time they were holding the completed Nativity quilt. "I can't believe we've found a photograph," Dora said, bumping fists with Julia.

"I didn't realize I had something so important to you," Julia apologized. "If you would have had this sooner, you wouldn't have had to stress so much."

"Don't fret. We managed to figure most of the puzzle out, anyway."

"Anything else of use?"

Dora flipped through the pages of the notebook. "The sketch book is filled with drawings of the quilt and its figures. Baby Jesus, the manger, the animals and everything are here," she exclaimed with joy. "The actual templates might be missing, but we have the sketches." She held the book to her chest. "There is one thing that bothers me."

"What is it?"

"Ellen Good is missing from the photograph. She was one of the quilters."

"Maybe she was busy or sick that day."

"Perhaps, but I believe there is more to this story."

Josie and Anthony arrived a week before Alexia's wedding. Dora thought back to the time she suspected Anthony of being involved in an art heist. Josie was in love with him and would not consider he could be a criminal. Anthony had lost weight and more hair since their trip to the west coast, and she could tell Josie chose his smart style clothing.

They were barely settled in before Milton took Anthony aside for a long chat, and Dora drove Josie down to the quilt venue to see the poinsettia quilt. Josie's eyes lit up with approval. "It turned out more beautiful than I expected."

"I have another surprise for you." Dora led Josie to the antique quilts and waited for Josie to notice.

"Is this your Nativity quilt?"

"No, it's the original one."

"Where did it come from?"

"We don't know. Someone brought it unnoticed. A note was attached, saying it was being donated to the quilters guild."

"And what about your Nativity quilt?"

"We're still in the process of completing it. Violet's mother had the templates for Jesus and the manger, although they are gone now. And get this," Dora's voice bubbled. "Julia bought a box of quilting miscellaneous at her estate auction. In the box were sketches of the patterns used, including baby Jesus and the manger."

"It's a miracle."

Dora nodded. "I asked Lana to help me complete my portion of the quilt. One more session should do it for us."

"You asked Lana to help?"

"I had to. You were gone, and I couldn't do it myself."

Josie hung her head. "Sorry, I was torn with staying or returning home."

Dora shrugged. "I'm hoping to have the Nativity quilt done and quilted before Christmas."

"How's Alexia coming with wedding plans?"

"I haven't gotten any panic calls lately, so I'm assuming all is going well except for the reception." Dora guided her toward Milton's trees. "We should stop by Julia's before we join the men. I barely had enough time to talk to Anthony."

Dora stopped in front of the wooden creations. "What do you think of Milton's trees?"

"Very imaginative. In fact, the entire venue is wonderful. The women came out in full force for this quilt show."

Dora drove them from the quilt venue to Julia's. Alexia's car was in the driveway. "We picked a good time," Dora noted.

Both Julia and Alexia embraced Josie as she entered the house. Alexia fussed over her aunts with cups of tea and Christmas cookies. "What can we help you with?" Josie asked.

Alexia pulled up a chair next to Josie. "We're pretty much set except for the reception."

Josie grimaced. "I'd consider the reception a major concern."

"What exactly do you have planned for the event? Dancing? Dining?" Dora asked after selecting a Russian teacake from the plate.

"John doesn't care for dancing, and a big meal isn't a priority, either. We discussed doing a simple cake, ice cream, coffee, and punch affair."

"If that's what you want, I'm wondering if you can use a portion of the quilt venue for a reception," Dora suggested.

Alexia wrinkled her brow. "How would that work?"

"The avenue of unique trees could be pushed back out of the way for the evening. Tables could be set up in the open spaces."

Josie raised her hand. "I've got an idea for tables. I know of a place where we can rent the old fashioned ice cream tables and chairs."

"We wouldn't be able to come up with enough," Julia commented.

"I'm sure we could find other small tables and chairs if we needed," Josie suggested. "Just think how cozy with quaint tables tucked in around the quilts would be?"

Dora frowned. "What about little kids and sticky hands." Daycare had taught her about that.

"The quilters may not appreciate us," Julia said.

Alexia smiled. "I like the idea. We'll rope out the area to be used."

"And watch the kids," Dora said wryly. "I've had experience in that department."

121

Milton urged Dora to find out all she could about Roger Duncan from Lana that afternoon when they met for their quilting session.

"Lana will not tell me anything especially if Roger Duncan was a wanted man."

Milton drew in a deep breath. "Aren't you interested in finding out why she is a recluse?"

"Yes, I'd like to, so I can help her, but I don't want to learn her dark secrets."

"Then there is no way of knowing unless Lana spills the beans."

"I must accept the way things are. If she wants me to know, she'll tell me." She detected that Milton was miffed at her, but he didn't understand how delicate the situation was. He left for the afternoon, so that the women could be alone.

Lana arrived around one o'clock. Dora had drawn out the templates from Prudence's sketch book. The rest of the scene had been finished except for baby Jesus and the manger. With no hitches, they should complete their portion that afternoon. Dora let Lana trace the first template on the fusible webbing before she asked about the cantata.

"I saw you at the cantata, Lana. Did you enjoy it?"

"You were right when you told me the music was spectacular. I can't say I understood it all, but yes it was pleasant."

Dora wanted to ask more, but froze at the thought of prying into her life. If only she could think of something innocent to ask. Finally, she had an idea. "Milton and I were at the cemetery the other day. My parents are buried there." She steadied her voice. "We happened to see your husband's gravestone."

"Yes, he's buried there."

"How long ago have you been without him?"

Lana's shoulders sagged. "A few years."

"Must be difficult. Milton and I have only been married a short time. If I lost him now I would be devastated." Suddenly, she felt the prick of remorse. She shouldn't have been short with Milton.

Lana dropped the baby Jesus template to her side. "I can't lie any longer."

Dora sat stunned. Lana had been lying?"

"I wasn't married to Roger. In fact, we had no relationship other than to use each other to achieve personal quests."

Dora remained silent, directing her full attention to her friend.

"It doesn't matter, anymore if I'm exposed as a fraud."

Dora felt the need to become involved in the conversation. "Why do you consider yourself a fraud?"

Lana's voice caught. "I wasn't married. If it wasn't for my cake business, I wouldn't know anyone."

"I'm sorry. What brought you here to Hedge City?" Dora prompted.

"Roger and I met at a friend's house in Omaha. My adoptive mother had just died. Before she passed on, she told me I originated in this area. I wanted to find my birth mother but was afraid to venture out on my own. Roger had gotten in trouble with the law. He had fallen on hard times and skimmed the profits from his Company. Luckily, they gave him the chance to pay back what he took. He wanted to make a fresh start with a new sales territory. We made a pact to help each other out and move to Hedge City. By then, I had become quite proficient at cake decorating."

"Have you found your birth mother?"

"No, I have no leads. Roger was no help." She daubed at her eyes with a Kleenex. "He spent little time with me."

"Milton is a detective. Perhaps he could help."

Lana's eyes widened. "A detective? I had no idea."

"There's no need to be afraid. From what you told me, you have done nothing wrong."

"Please keep what a tell you confidential. I shouldn't have said anything."

"We'll respect your wishes," Dora assured her. "Other than her general location, you have no more information on your birth mother?"

"No, I don't." Lana paused. "She may not even be alive."

"If you contact the adoption agency which handled your case, they can contact your birth mother. If she wishes to see you, she'll contact the agency, and they will give authorization for you to meet."

"I tried to, but I got nowhere."

"This is where Milton can help. With your permission, I'll speak with him."

"You're too kind. Why would you want to go to all this trouble for me?"

Dora blushed. "It's the right thing to do." She wasn't used to such compliments, but her heart sang with the possibility of uniting Lana and her mother. Hopefully, her mother was still living.

When Dora arrived home, she called for Milton as soon as she opened the door. Finding him in the living room, she apologized for irritating him, and he took her in his arms and said he was sorry for his impatience.

"Lana told me a few things this afternoon about Roger. They weren't married like you said." Dora shared all the information she had learned that afternoon. "She wants to find her birth mother, and I volunteered your services if needed." She smiled flirtatiously.

———

Dora offered to pick up Lana and drive her to the quilt guild meeting several days later. The quilt guild planned to meet for one last time to assemble the Nativity quilt. Dora intended to introduce Lana to every lady there in hopes she would make friends. Dora thought Lana seemed to have a new spring in her step and a new glow in her face. She prayed that the Holy Spirit was working in her life.

"Has Milton found out anything about the adoption agency?" Lana asked Dora as soon as she met her at the door.

"He advises you to contact them with a request to notify your birth mother."

"I'll do it after the meeting. I hope I get results this time."

"Good. If they turn down your request, Milton will see what he can do."

"I appreciate your help. I didn't know what to do, anymore. Life has become lonely and unbearable. If it wasn't for my cake business, life would have no purpose."

"I had no idea," Dora murmured. She couldn't even imagine what it would be like to be alone. She always had Josie and now Milton.

"We're here," Dora announced when they drove up to the community center. "Be prepared. I will introduce you to the members in hopes you will consider joining us." Dora did as promised and after introductions were completed, she joined in the Nativity quilt decisions.

"Our quilt won't look like the original," Faye commented. "Is that okay with you, Dora?"

"I didn't expect it to. Follow our original design and it will be perfect."

"Would you like to be the one to sew it together?"

"I can with assistance."

Dora and several of the guild members basted the sections together after consulting with one another on the adjustments needed. When the members finished the basting, Dora began the final stitching. They had decided beforehand the machine quilting would be left to another member.

The group's opinions divided on where the quilt should be displayed. Since the project had been Dora's idea, she was left to make the final decision. Not wanting to compete with the original quilt, Dora leaned toward displaying it in the church. The members agreed to her choice although they didn't think it would receive the exposure it deserved.

Darkness had descended on the town by the time Dora completed the quilt top. Even though, Lana received invitations to be driven home, she waited for Dora. Before they arrived at Lana's, Dora asked that she let them know what the adoption agency decided. Lana promised she would and waved to Dora as she left.

It had been a long day, and Dora was eager to get home and spend a quiet evening with Milton. Josie and Anthony had been invited out for supper which left them alone for a while. She mentally counted off the Christmas tasks waiting for her attention and was pleased she had survived all of them so far. The only major one left was Alexia's wedding. While she was basking in her accomplishments, she suddenly realized she hadn't bought Milton's Christmas gift yet.

The following day, the weatherman predicted a sunny and warmer day. Anthony and Josie planned to be gone all day Christmas shopping. After they left, Milton asked Dora if she wanted to drive out to Ellen Good's and see if she was at home. Since Dora had finished the quilts, she felt she had time but lamented she had nothing to take her.

"If Ellen isn't home, I suggest we notify the police," Dora said. "I don't trust that old man who lives in the cabin."

"Perhaps she's home, and we won't have to do anything that drastic."

As they approached Rock Falls, Dora was relieved to see smoke from Ellen's chimney and could hardly wait for Milton to stop the car. She beat Milton to the door and rapped several times before Ellen answered. "Dora, I didn't expect to see you again."

"We were by last week to bring you a tin of cookie, but you weren't home. We came by to check on you, but I'm sorry to say we ate all the cookies."

Ellen chuckled and opened the door. "Come in. I may have a few store-bought cookies to go with coffee." She motioned for them to sit up to the table while she poured coffee and opened a package of cookies that were sitting on the counter with several bags of groceries. By the looks of things, Dora surmised Ellen had just gotten back from where ever she went.

"We were worried about you," Dora told her in hopes she would tell them where she had been.

"I was visiting friends. I do that from time to time."

"We even stopped by the cabin occupied by an elderly gentleman," Milton added.

Dora glanced at him and frowned. She wouldn't have been so generous with Milton's description. "He wasn't about to tell us anything about you or where you were."

"That's Jasper. He watches out for me. Sorry if he was rude."

"No harm done," Milton said.

Dora opened her purse and took out the photograph of the Nativity quilt and its quilters and handed it to Ellen. "I found this in Prudence's things. My sister Julia bought a box of sewing items at Prudence's estate sale. This picture was amongst the items. I thought you might want to see it. It's a shame you weren't in it." Dora watched her reaction.

Ellen held the photo for a while studying it. "I was in Kansas City. The ladies finished the quilt without me."

"You'll never believe this, but the original quilt turned up at the quilt show. No one knows who brought it in."

"Really? No one saw who it was?"

"No. There was a note attached to it saying it was a donation to the guild."

"Unbelievable."

"You must come by and see it. It's displayed with the other antique quilts." Dora paused for a sip of coffee. "You said it was given to the minister. How could it find its way back to Hedge City?"

Ellen shook her head. "Did you finish your Nativity quilt?"

"We found sketches of the missing patterns in Prudence's estate items," Dora said. "I reproduced them on templates, and we finished the quilt top. A guild member is machine quilting it for us."

"Does it look like the original?"

"Similar. Lana Duncan helped me with the stable scene."

"I don't believe I know her. Who is she?"

"She hasn't lived in Hedge City long. She specializes in cake decorating."

Ellen folded and refolded her napkin. "Does she have a husband, children?"

"Neither. I have just come to know her. She's making my niece's wedding cake. I found out she quilted and since my sister Josie was gone and couldn't help me, I asked if she would assist."

"Interesting," Ellen murmured.

"If you would like to attend the quilt show, we'd be happy to come and get you and take you in to see it. Wouldn't we, Milton?"

"Yes, yes. It would be our privilege."

"Thanks for the invitation, but I don't want to trouble you. Jasper drives and he would take me if I wanted to go."

Dora couldn't imagine Jasper driving Ellen anywhere. Besides, both were recluses and weren't about to mingle with society.

"You're very thoughtful. Thank you, but it's unnecessary."

Seeing that Ellen wasn't interested in her invitation, Dora motioned to Milton that it was time to leave. She stood and smiled. "I'm relieved to see that you are okay and that you have someone to watch out for you," she said in all honesty.

"You're very kind." Ellen walked them to the door.

As Milton drove them away, Dora saw Jasper in the nearby woods, cutting down a tree. He stopped what he was doing and glared at them. Dora drew back from the car window. "I wonder what Ellen sees in such a strange man."

A light snow had fallen the next morning. Milton was out shoveling the walk, and Dora just finished the dishes when she received a call from a quilting member telling her the Nativity quilt was completed and ready for pick up. Dora invited Josie to go along and help her make a few decisions. At that moment she hadn't decided where to hang the quilt. While driving, Dora explained her quandary to Josie about where to display the quilt.

"The quilt show would be the best place," Josie said almost immediately. "Some ladies who worked on it attend different churches. They might be upset if the quilt isn't displayed in their church."

"Good point, but I don't want the two quilts in competition with each other while at the quilt show."

"But they won't be. The guild will not be awarding prizes will it?"

"No."

"Then what's the problem?"

"I suppose you're right. I didn't want people comparing the antique quilt with ours."

"Why don't you write up a little history of the original and explain your desire to make your own Nativity quilt," Josie said. "I think it's an interesting story."

Dora lifted her brows. "I could."

"Display the two photographs you found."

"Oh dear, I left the last picture with Ellen. I must drive out and get it."

"Let's drop the quilt off at the quilt show and take a trip to Ellen's. I'd like to get a look at Jasper." Josie snickered.

130

Dora frowned. "You would."

As soon as they saw the Nativity quilt, Dora gushed, "It's a painting masterpiece in fabric, the most important event in history. God's gift of Jesus to a sin filled world."

"Wow, Dora, I didn't know you were so emotional."

"Don't you feel it?"

"Yes. It means hope, joy, and eternal peace to me."

"I have another idea," Dora said. "Let's take the quilt to Ellen's and show her and then take it to the quilt show?"

"Do you think Ellen would appreciate you coming to visit again?"

"She's been friendly. Jasper? Not so much."

"Why is he protective of her?"

"I would like to find out, but she doesn't give us any clues."

As they pulled into Rock Falls, Josie kept on the lookout for Jasper. When she didn't see him, she groaned.

Dora laughed. "Are you disappointed?"

Josie scowled.

As Dora walked up to Ellen's door, she stopped and studied a set of footprints leading up to the house. Josie noticed, too. "Looks like a man's," she said to Dora. "Could it be Jasper?"

"Let's find out."

Josie tugged at her arm. "We should go. You don't know this Jasper fellow."

Dora ignored her plea, knocked, and waited. Ellen opened the door slightly and stepped outside. "Hello I... I have company," she said.

"Sorry to bother you, but I forgot the photograph of the ladies with the quilt. I came to get it and add it to the antique quilt display."

131

"Yes, I know where it is." Ellen hesitated. "Do you want to step inside the porch and wait?"

Dora was certain that Ellen didn't want them to see who was visiting. She thought if she could get inside the porch she might have a chance to see. "Yes, thanks," she said.

Ellen let them inside a small porch area. Then she opened the inside door, shut it, and left them alone. Seeing there was a window on the inside door, Dora crept over to it and peered in the window.

"Can you see anything?" Josie whispered.

"There's a set of men's boots inside the door."

"Jasper's?"

"Hard to tell. Here she comes." Dora hurriedly stepped back.

Ellen opened the door and handed Dora the photograph.

Dora thanked her and they left. "Good grief," Dora complained. "I don't have a reason to visit again. Otherwise Ellen will think I'm spying on her."

"I'm sure Jasper has already warned her."

Dora popped the steering wheel with her hand. "I forgot to show her the quilt."

Josie jumped. "Ah, Dora, we really didn't have an opportunity."

"No, we didn't. They're hiding something. Wish I knew what it was."

"You are really into this, aren't you?"

"Yes, I am."

As soon as they got home, Dora told Milton and Anthony about her visit to Ellen's. "Something is going on. I feel it."

"There's nothing we can do," Milton said. "They have done nothing we know of to break the law. They're just acting strange."

Anthony scratched his chin. "I'm ready for a case to solve. Sure, there isn't anything we could do, Milton?"

"I don't believe they're criminals, but I suppose you could do a background check. We don't know Jasper's last name. A few inquiries should give us something."

Anthony rubbed his hands together and smiled. "I'll begin right away."

Josie laughed. "He's been bored lately."

"While you two research, Josie and I will bake for the holidays." Dora reached for the recipe file while Josie donned an apron. "Let us know if you find anything."

Milton and Anthony divided the search tasks. Milton volunteered to visit the library, the school, and the knowledgeable bar tender he had visited once before. Anthony began with the computer search. While they researched, the ladies mixed up several batches of cookies. Soon the kitchen counters and table were filled with sugar and gingerbread cookies.

Several hours later, Milton came home just in time for supper.

Dora studied Milton's face. "Well," she said.

He grinned. "You're right to the point. I have something for us. I don't know if it's significant."

"Tell us anyway," Dora said.

"Ellen and Jasper were classmates. They may have known each other for years."

Dora set the roasted meat on the table. "I bet they are more than friends."

Josie winked. "If so why don't they live in the same house?"

Dora glared. "I don't mean it that way."

"How about you, Anthony? Did you discover anything?" Josie teased.

"They don't have a criminal record, and I can't find much on the internet."

Dora gestured for everyone to sit up to the table. "I just bet they have a secret they're sharing."

Milton passed the potatoes. "If only we could find out what it is."

―――

Alexia's wedding was the day after tomorrow. Dora and Josie rallied to Julia's call and offered assistance. The prairie church and the quilt show venue needed to be decorated. Dora and Josie volunteered for the church. Neither one wanted to carry in tables and chairs for the reception. Decorating would be minimal for the reception other than adding twinkling lights to the partition ropes and the head table. The quilts would provide the backdrop for the event.

Dora and Josie rode in Julia's SUV to the discount stores and flower shop and loaded the vehicle with poinsettias and evergreen swags. While driving to the church, they discussed the possibility the church would need to be cleaned again. Once inside they determined only sweeping and dusting were all that was required to bring it up to standard. After they completed these housekeeping chores, they decorated, according to Alexia's wishes.

Dora and Josie worked together to assemble evergreen swags for the window sills. Josie placed candle holders and red and gold candles amidst the greenery. Julia added red bows to the pews and then shook out a white lace tablecloth for the altar table. Fresh flowers and flameless candles were to be added the day of the wedding. The women placed a dozen poinsettia plants throughout the church. When the decorating was completed, they stepped back and admired the effect. "Beautiful," Julia commented. "Now let's stop at the reception venue."

Milton, Anthony, and a host of volunteers had moved in old fashioned ice cream tables and chairs that had been scoured from around the town and nearby neighbors. However, not all of them had been cleaned up for a wedding reception. Some needed a dusting and others that had set out on patios and decks required scrubbing. Dora feared Julia would collapse when she saw the condition of the tables and sent her home with Josie while she filled a pail with water and a scrub rag. Milton took pity on her and helped with the task. It was already dark when they finished. Dora sent Milton on his way home to start supper, explaining she had one more errand.

Dora had put in a full day, but she stopped at Lana's house to check on the cake. She knocked on the door and heard Lana's voice inviting her in. "Thought I'd stop by and see how the cake is coming."

Lana wiped her hands on a towel. "I'm baking the layers. Tomorrow I'll decorate. That's when it gets interesting. Sit down. I'll brew tea."

"It smells yummy in here." Dora was hoping Lana would ask her to stay for tea. She had been on her feet all day and was tired. Lana took another peek at her baking layers and sat down at the table with Dora.

"I have something to show you." Lana sorted through a stack of papers and produced an envelope. "This is from the adoption agency."

"Great news. What do they say?"

The teakettle whistled, sending Lana to the cupboard for cups. "The agency will contact my birth mother. If they don't hear from her in the specified amount of time, then they will assume she's not interested." Lana grimaced. "I must wait."

"Maybe your birth mother will answer right away."

"Or maybe not at all." Lana sat in the chair and crumpled.

"Have hope," Dora encouraged. "This probably isn't any of my business, but are you prepared to forgive her?"

"I've given it a lot of thought. She must be in her late seventies by now, and yes I'll forgive her."

"I'm glad to hear you are ready," Dora said. "Holding a grudge helps no one."

"I'm alone in this world, and I'm willing to risk developing a relationship with her if she'll let me."

"For your sake I pray she'll answer." Dora changed the subject and visited with Lana about the wedding cake.

Lana dried her eyes. "I practiced last night and saved the best poinsettias. Would you like to see them?"

Dora declined, claiming she wanted to be surprised. Since the supper hour was near, she bade Lana goodbye and drove home to one of Milton's surprise suppers. When she entered the door, she detected pork chops frying. Warm food for a weary body, she thought.

While they were eating, Dora told Milton the good news from the adoption agency. He was surprised that they responded so quickly. "Do you think it's someone from this area?" he asked her.

"That's the reason she came here. Her adoptive mother said she originated in this area although she was born somewhere else."

"You know all the elderly women. Who could be?"

She looked to the ceiling for answers. "There's Violet. She never married. Perhaps she had an affair although I highly doubt it. Berta was married and had children, but I suppose there was another life before marriage." Dora threw up her hands. "Any of the ladies in the rest home could be her mother."

"Will Lana tell you when she finds out?"

"She said she would. Just like her, we will have to wait."

The sun shone brightly on Alexia's wedding day, although it was to be an evening wedding, the brightness of the day carried over to everyone's disposition. Plans were progressing beautifully. The bride and her bridesmaids were off to the hairdressers while the groom and his groomsmen went bowling to relax their nerves. Julia checked her to-do list several times while her husband sacked out in his favorite chair.

All Dora and Josie had to worry about were making themselves presentable for the wedding and cutting the cake. Julia informed them to be at the church at four o'clock for pictures. All photo shots would be indoors, she told them. Julia also asked them if they would stop by the reception venue to ensure everything was in order. They dressed early to accommodate Julia's request.

Anthony and Milton accompanied the ladies while they inspected the reception venue. The tables had been covered in red and green Christmas tablecloths, twinkling lights added a festive aura, the punch bowl sat empty for the moment, and the wedding cake took center stage with its cascading poinsettias. "Lana did a super job," Josie gushed. "I hope it tastes as good as it looks." She attempted to dip her finger in the icing, but Dora slapped her hand.

Satisfied everything appeared perfect the two couples drove to the prairie church for pictures. Alexia and John and their wedding party were still outside posing for photographs before the sun set. Both Dora and Josie watched the setting sun's effect on the vintage bride and her attendants. "The dress and her flowers are stunning." Josie commented.

"The gorgeous woman inside the dress has something to do with it," Dora reminded her bluntly.

"Yes, of course."

The photographer called Dora, Josie, and their spouses into the church for the rest of the family pictures. An evergreen fragrance pervaded the church, causing Josie to sneeze. Alexia kissed her aunts and told the photographer she wanted a picture of her and her two aunts alone. After the traditional family portraits, the photographer grouped Alexia, Dora, and Josie together. "You look beautiful and we love you," both Dora and Josie said as she stuffed her Kleenex into her evening bag.

"Mom cried when she saw me in her dress."

"You've been a special daughter and a niece, too. We wish you a happy life." Dora embraced her, being careful not to crush her flowers. "Now don't cry," she said when she saw the beginning of tears. Josie, too, leaned in with a hug.

Alexia waved kisses and disappeared with her attendants in the ante room. Shortly afterwards, an usher escorted Dora and Josie to their seats with Milton and Anthony following. Accompanied by soft music, guests dressed in their finery filed in and fill the pews. The last to be seated were the parents of the bride and groom. Dora had never seen Julia look so elegant in a red and white tailored suit.

Ushers lit the candles at the altar, illuminating the red and white poinsettias and the greenery that Dora and Josie had carefully arranged. Shortly, the appearance of the groom and his attendants and the subtle change of music signaled the bridal procession was soon to follow. The two bridesmaids appeared in red and antique white street length dresses, carrying red and white flowers accented in white cascading ribbons. When the strains of the familiar wedding march played, all eyes turned toward the bride. Alexia, on her father's arm, beamed as she caught sight of her groom standing at the altar. Dora fumbled for a handkerchief in her purse, realizing Alexia had been more like a daughter than a niece. Josie reached for Dora's hand. Her eyes, too, were misty.

Dora immersed her attention to the traditional nuptials. It was only five months since she and Milton had committed to one another. Alexia and John had years together, but she and Milton remembered to thank God for every day they shared. She reached for Milton's hand and squeezed it. He returned her sentiment.

After the wedding, the bridal party left the church in an old-fashioned sleigh, a surprise gift from the groomsmen. The guests soon followed in cars where they could offer their congratulations and remain for refreshments. During the last week before the wedding, Julia had added sandwiches to the menu. Once the guests were seated, servers waited on them to keep traffic flow to a minimum.

Dora and Josie were standing at the punch bowl when Dora spotted Lana Duncan near the cake. She went over to her and thanked her for creating Alexia's wedding cake. "I wanted to see for myself if it arrived safely," she said.

"I came with it to make sure."

"Any news from the agency?" Dora whispered.

"Yes, they gave me the name."

Dora's eyes widened. "Who is it?"

"I'd rather not tell you here." Lana peered over her shoulder. "Please come by the house tomorrow."

Dora frowned. "Julia will need my help to clean tomorrow."

"Late afternoon would work."

"Okay. I'm anxious to see who it is. Someone I know?"

"I'm not sure."

"You'll stay for a piece of cake won't you?"

"I think not, but I want to remain until the Bride and Groom are photographed with the cake," Lana said. "I'll snap a picture to add to my albums.

"I don't think I have ever seen a cake so pretty," Dora said. "The red poinsettias spiraling down the white icing are stunning."

"It's easy to decorate with a Christmas theme."

Dora rested her hand on Lana's arm. "Please give me some pointers on cutting this wedding cake?"

Lana indicated where she should begin cutting after the bride and groom had their photo taken with the cake.

"Thanks. Josie and I have been nervous about doing it all wrong."

Milton approached Dora and took her arm. "We have a table waiting."

Dora extended another invitation to Lana to sit with them, but she turned her down.

As soon as they were near their table Dora whispered to Milton what she had found out. "Lana let me know the agency has told her who her birth mother is, but she wouldn't tell me tonight."

"She probably didn't want to upstage the evening. She'll tell you soon enough."

"True. She wasn't even sure I'm acquainted with her birth mother."

The reception with an ice cream parlor and quilt theme ended all too soon. John and Alexia were about to leave for their honeymoon but not without goodbyes to the family. Julia cried tears of joy. Dora and Josie struggled not to cry while they showed Alexia her wedding gift of the poinsettia quilt.

"For us?" Alexia inquired with disbelief.

"For you, our favorite niece," Josie said.

Alexia laughed. "I'm your only niece." She and John left the reception without the traditional shower of rice or bubbles only of fond good-byes.

"Where do they intend to live?" Anthony asked once they had gone.

"Right here in Hedge City," Dora said. "Alexia will continue with her daycare, and John will substitute teach until a position opens."

Anthony smiled. "And will you gals run the daycare until she comes back?"

Josie laughed. "Don't you remember? I'm going back to Iowa with you."

Dora shook her head. "My daycare days are over."

The next day, Julia had scheduled a clean-up morning. The men began with returning tables and chairs while the women stripped off the table cloths, carried out the punch bowl, and the few serving dishes. After the area was swept, and the trash taken out, they transferred to the prairie church.

"It's a shame to take down the decorations," Josie lamented. "The church will be alone, again."

"It was a pretty place for a wedding," Julia agreed. "The poinsettias will die if we don't' move them. But to where? Even if you take some, Dora, there are still too many."

Dora nodded. "The rest home. There are several ladies there that would just love holiday color."

"Great idea. And the greenery?"

"Let's take it, too. I bet we can use it outdoors somewhere. The residents might be allergic to it if we put it indoors."

When the church was cleared of the decorations, the ladies filled Julia's vehicle with the potted plants and greenery and stopped at the rest home. After getting permission, they brought in the poinsettias and distributed them among the residents. Dora reserved Berta and Violet for herself.

Dora left one in Berta's room. Since she was sleeping, Dora didn't disturb her. Violet, however, was wide awake and gasped when she saw the poinsettia. "For me?" she exclaimed.

"For you." Dora set the poinsettia, so she could see it.

"And how did your quilt turn out?" Violet asked.

"Very nice. Let me show you." Dora scrolled through the pictures on her phone and showed her when it was displayed at the quilt show.

Violet squinted. "Yes, I can tell it turned out well. I'm glad you could finish it."

"Finding the photograph and the sketch book was what I needed. Your mother didn't throw them away after all."

Dora explained that they were cleaning up after the wedding and had brought poinsettias to the rest home. She promised to visit again and then left to join her sisters.

The car still held a few poinsettias since Julia wanted to keep a few and take them to church for the candle light services to be held the next evening.

"Want to come with me to Lana's?" Dora asked Josie, hoping she would accept. Josie had always been her stabilizer.

"No, I'd be in the way. I'll have Julia drop me off at your house."

Dora was nervous but eager to hear what the agency found out concerning Lana's birth mother. Was it someone she knew?

Lana answered the door on the first knock. "I've been waiting for you all day."

"We finished with removing all the wedding decorations and the clean-up. I came as soon as I could. Is something the matter?"

"I'm not sure. I have the name of my birth mother. It's someone I do not know. She has a Hedge City post office box number, but I don't think I've ever seen her."

"Have you asked at the post office if they know where she lives?"

"I did. No one even remembers a woman picking up the mail."

"Odd. What's her name?" Dora asked after seating herself at the table.

"Ellen Good."

Dora's heart palpitated. "Ellen Good? I can't believe it."

"You know her?"

"I met her recently when I was searching for the original Nativity quilt patterns."

"Then you know where she lives?"

"I do. I've been to her place several times."

"Where is it?"

"She lives in the ghost town of Rock Falls."

"By herself? In a ghost town?"

"Yes, although there is a man who lives in the ghost town, too, and I think is a friend of hers."

"If she lives by herself then she must be of good mind and body."

"Yes, she is. It's about fifteen miles to her house. I could draw a map for you if you wish."

Lana hesitated. "I thought maybe you could drive me out there."

"Wouldn't you rather meet her alone?"

Lana grimaced. "No, I don't know what to say. If you already know her, it would be easier."

Dora thought of Jasper and his rudeness. If he was near he could dissuade the meeting.

"All right. I'll go with you. When do you wish to meet Ellen?"

"Tomorrow."

"She doesn't have a phone, so it might be a dry run if she isn't home."

"I'll chance it."

After their final plans were made, Dora drove home, praying all would go well for Lana.

———

"I wish you could come with me Milton. I don't relish meeting up with Jasper," Dora commented over morning breakfast.

"He's harmless. Remember we checked him out."

"I know, but he's intimidating."

"Just stand your ground. Use your teacher voice."

"Very funny."

He winked. "No, I mean it."

Dora finished her coffee and cleared the table before she picked up her purse and coat from the closet. "I'll be off, then."

Milton kissed her lightly. "Drive carefully. Give me a call if you need something."

"I need you," she said flatly.

Lana came out of her house, carrying a Christmas present and explained to Dora when she got into the car it was for Ellen. "After all tonight is Christmas Eve."

"How very thoughtful."

"It's just gloves and a scarf. Everyone can use a set." Lana cleared her throat. "Tell me about Ellen."

"I don't really know her, but now I might have an idea why she behaves strangely."

Lana grimaced. "Strangely? In what way?"

"She lives by herself in a ghost town. I'd say that was strange. I think it's because of her past."

"You mean me?"

"Possibly."

Luckily, the roads were free of ice and snow. In a half hour, they arrived at Ellen's where the smell of wood smoke surrounded her yard. Dora approached the door and knocked and then stepped back out of the way. Ellen answered and peered at Lana warily. "And who are you?"

Lana trembled at the question. Tears formed in her eyes. "I'm...your daughter."

Dora saw the resemblance even though Ellen was gray and her face wrinkled. Lana stood immobile until Ellen reached for her. They both wept in each other's embrace. Dora felt tears well up in her own eyes, suddenly missing her own mother.

Arm and arm Ellen and Lana walked into the living room where they sat down on the couch next to one another. Lana put the gift on the coffee table. Dora lagged uncertain where to go, eventually realizing they weren't even aware of her.

After tears were shed, Ellen explained to Lana that being an unwed mother was a terrible disgrace in the 1950s. "There was a lot of secrecy then, and my family pressured me to go away and give birth. "I was sent to my aunt in Kansas City. After the birth, you were whisked away to be put up for adoption. I've regretted that every day of my life."

Lana's shoulders slumped, and she broke down in tears, sobbing until Ellen folded her into her arms. Dora fought the lump in her throat. She couldn't help empathize with both mother and daughter.

When the emotional tears had been shed, Lana wiped her eyes. "Did you marry and have more children?"

"No, I didn't. I never met the right man, and without him I couldn't have children."

"A sad story."

"And your story?"

"My life was okay, but something was always missing."

"Would you like to meet your biological father?"

Lana startled and then scanned the room. "Where he is?"

"In the next room."

"I...I don't know if I'm ready for a father."

"We were both young then. He regrets the decision as much as I do."

"You two never married?"

"No, we didn't get along very well. Your father met someone else."

Lana's face tightened. "I suppose since he's here."

Both Lana and Dora gaped at Jasper when Ellen brought him in from the kitchen. He was taller than Dora remembered and still appeared shaggy and unkempt. Dora feared what Lana was thinking.

Jasper remained in the doorway, making no attempt for contact nor did he say anything.

Ellen frowned at him and then sighing she told them that Jasper lived alone in a cabin a quarter mile from her. Although they never married, they held a fondness for one another. When Jasper's wife died, he came looking for her. After finding her living alone, he built a cabin, so he could be near and care for her.

Ellen blushed, and Jasper shuffled his feet.

Dora thought it sounded like a love story but didn't ask any questions. She wondered how Ellen could care for a man who was offensive and uncouth. Dora knew the threesome had a lot to talk about and felt uncomfortable listening in. "Perhaps I should leave you alone and come back later."

Jasper cleared his throat. "We'll bring her back to Hedge City."

Dora jumped at the sound of his voice. She caught Lana's glance and saw she was okay with the plan. Without further explanation, Dora stepped outside, started her car, and left them alone to sort through the years they had been apart.

When Dora arrived home, she couldn't wait to tell Milton, Josie, and Anthony what had transpired. After Dora shared the details, Milton embraced her. "You've done a wonderful deed bringing a family together."

"I'm happy for them. Even Jasper was civil."

Milton laughed. "There's more to his story than we'll ever know."

"Lana may transform their isolated lives, and they will change hers," Dora said with hope. Seeing that everyone was dressed for the candle light services, she excused herself to get dressed all the while smiling to herself. She had never guessed that Ellen had given a child up for adoption. She marveled at how God worked his marvelous ways.

The church's interior was aglow with lit candles and soft music. With a thankful heart, Dora sat content among her family. She counted her blessings while squeezing Milton's hand.

Dora glanced to the left of the church uncertain what she saw. Ellen was almost unrecognizable in a dress. Her gray hair had been pulled into a bun. Jasper appeared to have taken a shower, clipped his beard, and wore a dated but clean sports coat and jeans. Lana sat between them beaming. Dora rejoiced in seeing them together and hoped she could have a word with the newly reunited family before they left.

When the service concluded, Dora stepped quickly to where she had seen Lana. She called to them. Ellen slowly turned around and smiled. "We stopped at the quilt show before we came to the church. I wanted to see the Nativity quilt on display." Ellen looked at the floor. "I want you to know it was I who brought the quilt back to Hedge City."

Dora's eyes widened. "You?"

"I was gone to visit Pastor Helms's daughter when you came by to call on me. She's had the quilt since her parents died. You see, I corresponded with the family for years. They were the only ones who didn't shun me." Ellen smiled mischievously. "I knew where the quilt was all along."

Dora held her hand over her heart. "I had no idea it was you. Why did you bring it back?"

"You wanted it so badly."

"Helms's daughter didn't mind giving it back?"

"No, it doesn't have much meaning to her."

Dora smiled and reached for her hand. "Thank you for bringing it home."

Lana grinned with news. "Ellen and Jasper have asked me to make their wedding cake."

"Really? I mean Congratulations," Dora stuttered. "Will it be soon?"

"On Valentine's Day."

Dora wished them a Merry Christmas and rejoined her family. Milton pulled her aside. "Dora, you look positively radiant. What's up?"

"I'm happy. This has been the best Christmas ever."

The Christmas season had been busy, unlike her original plans. But tonight Dora wouldn't change anything. She had discovered vintage quilt patterns from a Nativity quilt that sent her on a journey of discovery, not only for herself, but others as well.

She along with her sister and friends shared fellowship in crafting two Christmas quilts. The poinsettia quilt was a gift for her niece Alexia's wedding, and the Nativity quilt started a spiritual awakening in her life and led her to the lonely and the lost.

And there was more. She and Milton deepened their relationship. Each new discovery about one another expanded their love.

But most importantly, by searching for the Nativity quilt and showing love for others, Dora recommitted herself to the Lord, the heart and essence of Christmas.

Printed in Great Britain
by Amazon